LOOSE LEAVES

Unbound Press Literary Competition Anthology
Volume 1

Loose Leaves:
Unbound Press Literary Competition Anthology
Volume 1

An Unbound Press Book: ISBN 978-0-9558360-9-1

First published in 2010 by Unbound Press
3/1, 54 Hughenden Lane, Glasgow, G12 9XJ

www.unboundpress.com

Cover Design by Spilling Ink Review
www.spillinginkreview.com

Preface

This preface is simply a way of saying thank you to all those who entered our competitions, and congratulations to our prize-winners and runners-up, in this inaugural year of the Unbound Press Literary Competitions. We chose a range of different genres in order to present a varied read in this anthology – but even then, we were amazed and gratified by the sheer diversity of material entered in each category.

In order to showcase as much writing talent as possible in a single volume, we chose the runners-up purely on merit, rather than choosing a set number for each category.

The non-fiction entries in particular were a revelation – this was without doubt the strongest category overall, although not the most popular.

The biggest disappointment was the fact that we had to rule out a number of excellent 1st chapter of a novel entries, simply because they had previously appeared online – despite the fact it was made clear in the rules that this was not acceptable. We are looking for the fresh and new, so anything that has been freely available to view on the internet – even on a personal blog – had to be discounted.

We will be running a further batch of competitions next year, with some new categories – on the grounds that variety is the spice of writing!

Here it is, then, Loose Leaves Volume 1. Enjoy!

Nicola Taylor

Other Unbound Press Publications

NOVELS

Annabel	Elon Whittaker
French Sally	William Prince
Unreasonable Force	Charlie Taylor
Year of the Ginkgo	Sharon Dilworth

SHORT STORIES

That's What Ya Get!	Brindley Hallam Dennis
The Journey and Other Stories	Charlie Taylor
By Invitation Only	Various

NON-FICTION

Circe's Island	Isabel Gillard
The Scottish Wedding Planner	Nicola Taylor

Contents

Short Story: 1st Prize
Judy Walker

All There Is

I hand Liz my plastic carrier bag, which contains three thermos flasks and a foil parcel. We were all asked to bring a specified part of the menu – mine was the starter. Sort of a potluck supper but with the luck element taken out.

'It's soup – stilton soup – and bread.'

'Lovely! So….?'

I realise she is awaiting further instruction. 'It just needs warming – but don't boil it, it's got cream in.'

'And the bread?'

'Just warm it in the oven.'

'For how long?'

She's not a cook, Liz. She waves me through to the lounge and disappears into the kitchen.

I've been looking forward to this girls' night, but now I am here I feel awkward, as though I've arrived in evening dress when everyone else is wearing jeans.

The three others are already installed on two pale sofas. Patty is revealing that the trousers she is wearing are from H&M's children's department.

'They were for age 13 and, even better, they were on buy one get one free, so Emily got the other pair.' Having delivered her punch line with glee she sips her wine and sits back, ready to relish the reaction.

Predictably, everyone marvels. I think of the time I tried to get my son's jeans on – we're the same height – and they got stuck at my thighs.

Liz is back. 'Is it the kind of bread that needs butter?'

I begin to wonder if she's taking the piss.

Now we're hearing about how Val got a pair of £60 boots, that were already marked down to £49, for £35 because she managed to find a tiny little mark on them. Then, when they went to the loo in John Lewis, her daughter didn't come out for ages because she'd started her period – very first one – and Val didn't have anything with her and the machine was out of order but luckily a lady there realised the problem and gave her a pad that she happened to have in her handbag.

Pilgrim through this barren land. The words just come into my head and the tune of my favourite hymn threads its way through the chatter. I think I may be humming out loud so I take a handful of crisps, which clatter between my teeth. I know my cheeks are red and I hear my mother's voice: 'You sound like a horse, Shirley.'

I try to swallow them down quickly but I haven't chewed them up small enough and one gets caught in my throat, causing me to cough violently. A piece of crisp shoots out of my mouth and lands on the polished coffee table. Everyone has seen it. No one mentions it.

I am weak.... I take a tissue from my bag and wipe my mouth and watering eyes.

Jackie's daughter has spent a night in hospital with suspected appendicitis and the staff all said she was a delight and when the doctor arrived he was in his scrubs and he was drop dead gorgeous and called Salvatore. I start to say that my son had a similar problem but I give up because I don't think anyone hears me as they are onto Patty's daughter's broken finger now. Apparently she can still play the trumpet, although she can't write.

I listen and smile, listen and laugh. I think that's the right thing to do. My ears go funny and the conversation sounds far away. I sit very still and wonder if I am really here, in this room. I hold my breath for a minute, then let it out again. I give my arm a little shake and think about the time at school when I was told off for interrupting the teacher by asking a question.

Strong deliverer, strong deliverer.

Jackie looks over at me. 'Are you all right?'

'Yes, fine thanks. Just…' Did she hear me? Did I say it out loud?

The dog waddles in. It's a fat, shaggy thing with a tail that looks like a hairpiece pinned on to its arse. I don't particularly like dogs but I loathe Toby. He makes straight for the bowl of crisps.

'No Toby! Oh, who's a bad boy then?' Liz fawns over him and proceeds to tell us, whilst hugging his gormless face into her and – yuk, kissing it – how naughty he is but how she loves him to bits – they all do. I've never actually seen her or either of her daughters walking Toby. That's Roger's job. That would be Roger who I remember saying that if they got a dog he would leave. That would be Roger who, when asked by Liz to admit that he secretly adored Toby and would miss him if they didn't have him, cited the two hours he savoured every six weeks when Toby was at the dog parlour being shampooed and clipped.

Dinner's a long time coming. We've admired each other's hair and clothes, talked about Jackie's forthcoming holiday-of-a-lifetime to Australia (the itinerary for which she has planned down to the last photo opportunity) and indulged in a little light gossip about a couple we all know who are splitting up.

We eat, finally, in the garage, which has been converted into a poky… well, dining room, I suppose; although, curiously, it has a Belfast sink at one end and a wardrobe at the other. Liz makes a deprecating joke about the garage thing, in the same way that she does about only using the back door so visitors have to troop in through the kitchen. She has a perfectly good front door, which opens into a lovely hall. I am puzzled as to why this access is never used but more puzzled as to why she finds it so funny to say they never use it and how badly they treat their guests, making them use the tradesmen's entrance.

The soup is served tepid. It looks grey and gruel-like in Liz's white china soup plates, instead of pale and creamy as it had when I was making it; but everyone says it's lovely. I should have brought some parsley to garnish it. My homemade walnut bread, nestling in a linen napkin, looks too dark, like thick brown paint on a child's picture. I take a piece and bite into it. It disintegrates into dry crumbs in my mouth. I'd like some butter with it, but it's up the other end of the table.

Bid my anxious fears subside.

If I just keep myself focused on that hymn, it will be all right, I tell myself and I look at the butter once more, but it hasn't moved.

Talk moves on to children again. It's like one of those ghastly Christmas round robin letters but in 3D. Each takes a turn at citing their children's latest achievements, which are listened to attentively and congratulated appropriately. I consider telling them that my son has a mentor now who makes sure he goes to lessons, sits with him to check he's working properly and that he writes down his homework tasks so I can see that he does them. I imagine their reactions. They would make sympathetic little noises in their throats as I spoke, then there would be a short silence before Liz and Jackie, probably, would voice encouraging remarks. I ladle up my soup and listen to the chatter.

Roger comes in to pour more wine for us and clear the table. I look round the table at these women, who are my friends, and wonder why I feel so apart from them. They are clever and funny and well dressed and slim. I look at them very carefully but I don't see any rolls of tummy fat or grey hairs. I tug my blouse down and pull my stomach in. They eat salads and lots of fruit and they never keep biscuits in the house. They don't chomp Snickers bars in the car or scoff bags of crisps in front of the telly and when the chocolates are passed round later, they will all say no. I clench my fingers into the palms of my hands under the table and then look to see if I've broken the skin.

It's a comfortable, happy evening, with lots of fun and laughter. I want to enjoy it, I *desperately* want to enjoy it. It seems so easy just to chat about things; all sort of things. But what is the point of it? Where is the meaning in it? How does chat move anything on? I can feel my soul longing, reaching through my mind for the desire, the real joy-giver, I know is there but, like a half-remembered dream in the morning, is just, tantalisingly, beyond my grasp.

We are back in the lounge now with coffee and Toby is dragging his bottom along the carpet. Liz berates him ineffectually and he responds by exposing his penis. I feel a strong urge to kick him – and her. *Guide me…*

We're talking about the shortage of plumbers and how ridiculous it is to expect 50% of the population to go to university.

'Especially when you can get a degree in media studies or something at a polytechnic that calls itself a university,' I say. *Guide me, O...* 'Where's the academic rigour in that?' No-one is joining in but I carry on. 'I mean who would think that was worth anything?' They all look at me and I begin to panic, my confidence down to a trickle. *Death of death, and hell's destruction.* 'I wouldn't, I know that.'

There is a moment's silence and then they carry on talking; pretending, as if I had farted, that they haven't heard me. Is this it, then? Is this all there is? I slide the material of my blouse up my arm to glance at my watch and look forward to going home, having a bath, thinking things through. Maybe it's me after all.

I start humming: *Guide me, O thou great Redeemer,* it's my favourite hymn, and Liz says Roger's rinsed out my thermos flasks.

Essay: 1st Prize
Seif El Rashidi

Four Aces

'*Quatre As,*' a waiter announces, serving Caroline. There are few surprises at the Gezira Club; standards slip and slowly the old aristocracy fades, but year in, year out, the menu remains unchanged. The veal may be a little tougher now, and on crowded summer nights, many a jug of lemonade is returned to the kitchen almost untouched. 'Coloured water,' disgruntled members complain. I have recently discovered card games, and eye Caroline's dinner with interest, wondering what exactly the four aces are meant to be. Suddenly, I have card-game jargon on the brain. Except for my father, a regular, we are here for my friend to meet his boss's mother-in-law. 'Jasper is clever,' someone had stated earlier. Playing his cards right, I had thought, only then realizing the meaning of the phrase.

That evening, Jasper had called. 'The Gezira Club at nine,' he had suggested, unenthusiastically. Too polite to turn my father's invitation down, he was trying to entice a youngish crowd. I conceded easily, but expected an evening that was dreary at best.

'There will be singing and dancing,' my father had promised at our kitchen table a week earlier, as he extolled the virtues of several club members. I knew those club dinners well. There was indeed a singer who appeared in summer, singing old French favourites until the increasingly Arabised crowd demanded Egyptian classics. The dancing, though, was usually limited to Guido, an Italian-Egyptian whom I barely knew, but who represented an erstwhile cosmopolitan Egypt, alive only in the minds of dreamers like myself.

'Shall I wear a suit?' Jasper had asked, a question I had found absurd, until it dawned upon me that the club, now rather dowdy, maintained an illustrious reputation. Awaiting the arrival of my three British friends, I looked around, scrutinizing the area we referred to simply as 'the dinner'. Will they enjoy it? I wondered doubtfully while selecting a table, taking the surroundings in, as if for the first time. The members were predominantly old, many unashamedly inelegant, but respectable. The tablecloths were reasonably clean, the glasses matched each other, and the lawn, though yellow by British standards, was in good shape considering the heat. Our dinner companion, Madame Esmat, was upper-crust. Well-educated, multilingual and articulate, she was unimpressed by our waiter, who answered her questions vaguely, exemplifying the incompetence of the average Egyptian, she thought.

The rest of our party eventually arrived, and trundled in solemnly, except for Caroline, who was bursting with energy, as always. She later toyed with ordering a Chef's Salad, unaware that there was only one type of salad there, and that it was tasteless. With some encouragement from my father, she finally opted for the breaded veal dish whose name intrigued me.

Isabelle, a friend of Jasper's who had worked in Jerusalem, was poised but preoccupied. A bomb had exploded in Israel that night, and her boyfriend, a Palestinian, lived there. She left early to meet other friends, after having come across as 'refined', an epithet my parents use sparingly.

'I'd like to dance,' says Caroline enthusiastically after dinner.

'Then dance,' I reply, with a total lack of enthusiasm.

I immediately feel slightly idiotic as Abu Heif, recently chosen as the best swimmer of the twentieth century, and now in his seventies, walks off with Caroline in his arms.

'I'll dance if we change the venue,' I mutter later, at one of Caroline's increasingly infrequent interludes at the dinner table. By now a crowd has formed to watch her; she is brilliant, and Tante Samiha, the famous mother-in-law that Jasper has come to meet, assumes that Caroline can only be Lebanese. My father, thoroughly enjoying himself, dances incessantly with surprisingly agility.

'Who is that you're with?' someone asks him.

'A friend of my son's,' he replies, as the rest of us remain seated.

Jasper eventually charms my mother and leads her to the dance floor, in reality just an illusion, the patch of grass closest to the singer. Only Madame Esmat and I are left at the table, but soon join the others. We move rather slowly; Madame Esmat is my grandmother's age and, as it later transpires, she is dancing to annoy Tante Samiha, whom she dislikes.

I finally get to dance with Caroline – by this point, a star. She simplifies her steps to match my ineptitude, which gives me confidence. I forget the onlookers, the tablecloths, and the yellow lawn, and begin to enjoy myself.

Later, we walk over to La Bodega, where Jasper is to meet a British diplomat. Among Cairo's trendy crowd, La Bodega is in. It is plush, new and expensive, and its patrons, unlike those of the Gezira Club, are image conscious. Caroline saunters in, welcomed like an old friend. She has been here but a week. Thanks to her, the bouncer calls me prince, an unusually high title, even in Cairo, where for a small tip anybody can become a lord, momentarily.

Seated in the lounge, we talk of over-confidence. The lighting is dim, the conversation engaging. While we chat, stunning young ladies sip cocktails elegantly, without pretension. This is Cairo's new Gezira Club and, one day, it too will fade. Perhaps twenty years from now I will meet Caroline in England and she will ask me about the place.

'Oh, it closed down long ago,' I will say, remembering her amazing dancing by the fireplace in the foyer. Or maybe La Bodega will remain and today's yuppies will become middle-aged habitués, unaware that times have changed and that they are no longer cool. 'Your sister was here yesterday,' the waiter will tell me, as I lead a rebellious teenage son of Jasper's, whose middle name is bound to be Heber, to my table.

Caroline, Jasper implies, is showing off. I disagree, thoroughly impressed by her lack of inhibition. She has taken Cairo by storm; at dinner, her exuberance eclipsed Jasper's charm, hence his disapproval. The implication troubles her and we discuss it at length while Jasper wanders off in search of a phone card. Introverts, we conclude, are no less modest than anyone else. Besides, Caroline is outgoing, a plus. I try to reassure her, yet she seems unconvinced.

The music distracts Caroline, and a young man in tight jeans, whom my mother would have only described as 'not correct', asks to dance salsa with her. She disappears excitedly behind the curtain separating the lounge from the vestibule, leaving her green, bubble-gum-flavoured drink behind.

Jasper, back from his quest for a phone card, and myself recall the Gezira Club dinner, chuckling freely over its most amusing moments; we are good friends and with nobody to impress, we can be ourselves. The conversation soon turns to writing, a subject for which Jasper has both a passion and a talent.

'They won't find a better writer,' he says matter-of-factly, speaking about himself. His remark is simply stated, totally lacking smugness. There is no sense of accomplishment here, nothing boastful in his tone of voice. It is a succinct and earnest comment by a fledgling journalist who thinks he's the best.

I was later to remember the king in Exupery's *The Little Prince* who, from a planet the size of a watermelon, spoke with 'magnificent simplicity', believing that he controlled the universe. Yet, truth is, Jasper did in fact write brilliantly. To his peers, his piece on the suicide of a former schoolmate, the prince of Nepal, may have seemed self-promoting. But if, at the back of some old desk drawer, they were to find a clipping of the article, unsigned, and removed from its front-page spot, and were to read it for what it was, it would come across as a well-written and meaningful reflection on life by someone mourning the death of a friend.

Dancing replenishes Caroline's energy; beaming, she returns to find me admonishing Jasper for his over-confidence. She joins in, hesitantly at first, but soon we are picking Jasper's six-word statement to the bone. Armed with a handful of quotations, the fruits of a public-school education, he attempts to defend himself, but even Orwell and Proust cannot help him justify his inflated ego.

A thought enters my mind; I try repeatedly to suppress it, but fail, and in a rare moment of competitiveness, I decide to challenge Jasper. Always cautious, I offer to write a story comparable to his. Nonchalantly, Jasper calls my bluff, sure that he can trump me. Caroline slaps the table with elation. Surprised at my challenge, which makes even Jasper seem modest, she appoints herself judge.

The subject is agreed upon: our evening. I realize that this will require strategy, plans within plans. I could flatter the judge by describing her radiance, or perhaps her stunning cornflower-blue eyes. But that would be too obvious, and futile, for Jasper is renowned as the flatterer par excellence. Praising my competitor might also work; I make a mental note, and re-reading my essay a few weeks later, shrewdly change my description of Jasper's writing from very good to brilliant.

Above all, a lucid account of the Gezira Club is likely to impress. I could mention the horse races, the sweet-scented but mouse-infested bales of hay, the horses with their names crudely embroidered on their jackets. Who would know that I hadn't set foot there for years? Maybe also the running track, with its middle-aged ladies who strut in high heels clutching their handbags and then return to feast on canapés and crème caramel and gossip. Yet Jasper is bound to describe better, using words like elfin and argot. Besides, descriptions would clutter a text already replete with thoughts and digressions.

A good anecdote might do the trick, like the story of the peroxide blonde with fuchsia lipstick who called for *jihad*, holy war, against Israel. 'Go and fight yourself,' two men retorted, mesmerized by Hello magazine, 'and leave us to admire Catherine Zeta-Jones.'

The possibilities are countless, and the challenge thrilling. I have missed my calling as an architect, and know that tomorrow's Millennium Bridges and Getty Museums will not be mine. If only for an evening, writing can mirror the process of design, allowing me to refine and streamline a rough idea to near-perfection. Ands and buts and alsos are to be my corridors, my passageways; the Gezira Club, my cornerstone. Through reading and re-reading, my work will become dangerously familiar and, immersed in it, my eye will slacken. Like architectural critics stumbling on a poorly-placed step, Caroline and Jasper will come across an extra comma and pause. Frowning, they'll tackle the sentence again; Caroline puzzled, Jasper gleeful.

Jasper will write profoundly; provided he steers clear of science fiction and ghost stories, his essay will be a gem. There will be no linguistic errors, no awkward sentences. His descriptions, always poetic, will be detailed but never verbose. Yet, inevitably, he will feign displeasure, fussing incessantly over a minor fault, thereby emphasizing the overall excellence of his work. For him, success must be effortless, and he will tell us that, overworked and lacking sleep, he has written his story in under an hour. Almost convinced, and expecting something half baked, we will begin to read a highly polished and masterly account, possibly his best.

I look forward to our contest, yet something troubles me. It is not the challenge, nor the fact that I have relentlessly harassed a friend. Deep in thought but still attentive to the buzz at La Bodega, I hear the chatter of a jovial crowd. They burst in from behind the curtain; highly spirited, they spot Caroline, who jumps euphorically to her feet. In a sentence, she describes our evening.

'The Gezira Club!' her friend Fafi exclaims, 'I've been a member since 1929.' Fafi, like the rest of us, is under thirty.

'It's Thursday,' they remind us, 'Party night.' Suggesting a livelier venue, they urge us to move on. The idea is enticing, and relishing it, we promptly pay the bill. I look forward to coming home at dawn, the sign of a Thursday night well-spent.

Outside La Bodega, taxis linger. Oblivious to the swanky cars and valet parking, they foolishly await the yuppie crowd. While the others squeeze into Fafi's silver Polo, I mumble something about a fictitious early-morning appointment and then quickly disappear. Aghast at my newly-discovered arrogance, I rush home.

Flash Fiction: 1st Prize
Gill Hoffs

It's considered unlucky to kill them ...

No-one noticed at first. 'Phobes slept a little easier, venturing into garden sheds and other previously forbidden areas, able to breathe minus paper bags.

But the flies. Oh God, the flies.

Shimmering seas of translucent wings, a background drone of insect tinnitus, creamy grubs in every mouthful of food. Some profited, as is always the way. Haberdashers sold out of netting, factories switched from cosmetics and other useless luxury items to the two boom industries; mesh and insecticide. Streets had the appearance of a cheap Hallowe'en, the residents scurrying in shrouds through a midgy miasma.

Jobseekers now perform Human Services to receive benefits, wielding plastic flippers in a dervish dance, swatting wherever they go, scraping the minute carcasses into biohazard containers strapped to their waists, hoping to annihilate sufficient volume to win bonus benefits.

Asthmatics and allergics soon died out, eliminated by vile clouds of insecticide sprayed by desperate citizens.

Frogs became coveted creatures, special patrols guarding clusters of their spawn, the pale gelatinous grapes worth more than comparably sized pearls. The rich and powerful keep their own in special jewelled harnesses about their bodies. Offices have their water coolers adapted as host ponds to attract staff. Australia grew into a lead nation purely by exporting their once reviled cane toads. It's now a capital offence to harm or even permit harm to be done to frogs, toads, swifts, or their domains. A six year old boy was hanged for damaging a swifts' nest while bouncing his ball off a wall. Herons and other frog-eating birds command a high bounty.

New towns are developed in a reverse of historic principles; wind tunnels coveted and marshes made frog-friendly. Instead of once common white lights, people have adjusted to blue and purple electro-killers illuminating their homes and workplaces, whole walls glowing with promised death, businesses paying artists to shape their names into the mortal coils. High season changed in the tropics from the sunny still days of old Hollywood films, to hurricane and monsoon months.

Lifting aside the already crowded curtain of flypaper (changed hourly) to enter the church, I paused by the font to bless myself and its attendant frog, then swished into the depths. Huge moths fluttered round my hand, brownly mocking angels, as I paid the priest for a taper.

Lighting citronella candles, I mourned the death of spiders.

1st Chapter of a Novel: 1st Prize
Louise Hume

The Beginners' Guide to Parenting

'I hate weddings, don't you?'

The man in front of me slams coins into the cigarette machine as if it's all its fault. His suit is tight in all the wrong places and can hardly contain him as he stoops to yank the packet out of the drawer. The jacket's got a ridge on the shoulder, like it's spent years on a coat-hanger, and the trousers show half an inch of sock at the bottom. I can tell he's wearing the suit grudgingly, like a footballer at an awards ceremony, or a TV gangster – someone whose body's made for running and kicking and beating the hell out of other people. He pulls a cigarette out of the packet with his teeth and offers it to me. I don't smoke but I take it just to feel the shock of his fingers against mine. As he steps closer to light it for me, thick strands of black hair tumble into a face that looks as if it's been chiselled by a great sculptor who just ran out of time. Nose slightly too big, mouth a smidgen wide, chin that looks as if it needs a bit chipped off. Together, these imperfections add up to an accidental sort of handsomeness. To me it's nothing short of spectacular and I've been wanting to get my hands on it through every single minute of this long, long wedding, which being French, started at ten this morning and probably won't stop until halfway through next Wednesday. I spent the entire ceremony at the *mairie* watching his dark, restless head out of the corner of my eye, itching to bury my fingers in his hair. During the *vin d'honneur* I imagined sweeping the champagne glasses off the table and pinning him onto it, and when he danced with one of the bridesmaids, only a conversation about a sideboard that looked like a late piece by Ruhlmann with my French brother-in-law, who's also the bridegroom, prevented me dragging her away by her hair extensions.

Now, at last, we face each other outside the *salle des fetes* in the corridor that leads to the toilets, and I wonder if he can tell what one-track programme of filth is running in my head. He's giving nothing away. Like his hair, his eyes are as dark as night and as impossible to read.

'Weddings are alright,' I say. 'They have their good points. Free booze. Opportunities to do things you wouldn't normally do, things you end up regretting…'

'But things that are fun at the time?'

He steps closer to allow the bride's aunt who's in a wheelchair to get to the ladies. Behind the odour of vodka, his breath smells of mints. It's unexpected and cute. He pulls one of the hairpins that are holding together my improbably neat tower of hair and puts it into his pocket. I slide my finger down his tie. The knot looks like one you'd find holding fishing lines together.

'Terrible choice, that tie,' I say.

'All ties are terrible choices, but you've got to wear one if you're best man.'

'But… pink!'

'Do I look gay?'

'You just look like a drunk man in an awful tie. How many have you had, anyway? I bet you can't walk in a straight line. See those pedaloes on the lake out there? Bet you can't get there without falling over.'

This is a ruse to get him outside, away from the guests who keep bustling past and asking why we aren't enjoying the dessert course, that the *petits-fours* are made by a pastry-chef who once made a cake for Johnny Depp.

It's dark outside. The pedaloes are tucked behind the floodlit pavilion of the *salle des fetes,* stacked up, waiting for the families who'll flock to the lake tomorrow if the weather's good.

He walks in a straight, if slightly slanted, line and suddenly produces a champagne bottle out of his jacket and two glasses. They're not proper champagne flutes, just tumblers that he's swiped from the children's table. He holds them up like trophies and beckons me towards him.

'Ever had sex in a pedalo?' he asks as I join him. His hand slips unceremoniously around my waist and makes its way downwards. He pulls me closer and his breath on my neck feels like a silk scarf that someone's slowly sliding over my throat.

'You're going to have to try harder than that,' I lie, stifling a laugh.

'No, I don't.' There's a pop. Somehow he's uncorked the bottle with one hand. 'I'm French. Romance is part of my national character.'

'Romance? Is that what you're calling it?'

He pulls me closer, flattening my breasts against his massive chest. His fingers smell of spilled champagne and I put one in my mouth and suck.

'And I'm so glad promiscuity is part of yours.' He's walking me backwards now, manoeuvring my leg with his into one of the pedaloes that's tethered to the edge. I'd gladly somersault into it if it means any more of this but decide to rack up the tension by stumbling a bit as if I don't know what he's trying to do, what his intentions are. His mouth's on mine now, his lips pinching mine, his tongue sliding into my mouth. It's all I can do not to slither out of his arms but I soon feel the floor of the little boat wobble, the plastic of the seat against my back. As I open my eyes, I notice the prow is a cartoon duck, its cheerful grin in the moonlight takes on a saucy glint.

There's a splash as the tumblers fall into the lake.

'Shit!'

The boat rocks violently as he crashes next to me, puts his leg between mine, yanks up my dress.

'Wait,' I say.

'What for?'

'It's the tie. Sorry.'

With one gesture, the tie's overboard. It floats on the surface like a snake, uncoiling then disappearing into the blackness.

'Now,' he says and I feel his hands under my back, my legs around his waist, those stupid shiny high-heels I paid too much for and will probably never wear again, stuck above his head like a rude gesture. Strands of his hair fall into my eyes.

Afterwards we sit in silence curled together as the pedalo rocks gently to the rhythm of the lake. I kiss his head which is nestled on my shoulder.

'Why can't they all be like our wedding?' he says. 'Quick, to the point, and with more chips.'

'There were only chips at our wedding, Eric,' I remind him. 'Our reception was one of the chip stands on Dieppe seafront and there was only the two of us.'

'What more do you want?'

'Nothing, absolutely nothing. It was the best day of my life. What would I want with Johnny Depp's pastry chef?'

'That's what I love most about you, Karen.'

'What?'

'Your total disdain for Johnny Depp's pastry-chef.'

From the *salle des fetes* there's a steady stream of chatter, some laughter. They must have started the speeches. Against the slow, steady lapping of the lake it sounds like a laughter track from some distant TV set. I feel like we could be a million miles away, the darkness enwrapping us like a big, comfy duvet. By day Lake Caniel is as bright as a cartoon and just as subtle. There are ducks, canoes for hire, neat paths, hot-dog huts, ice-cream stands, a make-do beach with sand that's brought in by lorries, and a constant happy buzz that always makes it feel like Sunday afternoon. I think about how, just a few years ago, before Eric tumbled into my life as the subject of an article I was writing as a journalist on the local paper in Brighton (the article was called *City Bin Shock! Why the Seafront Bins Aren't Being Emptied* and Eric was the luminous-vested council employee who'd been found smoking a joint with his arm around a blonde in a bikini behind a sandwich bar, his empty trolley and broom parked beside him), I didn't know Lake Caniel, the ice-cream stands and the winking duck pedaloes existed. Probably then, if I thought about the future at all, it would have contained the same uncoordinated flurry of articles about council meetings, school pantomimes and badly-funded OAP day-centres, the same basement flat at the wrong side of the Brighton-Hove boundary, and the getting up-going to work-staying out too late-getting up-going to work narrative as it always had. I'd never have known that life could be about quick, fumbly and frankly quite clumsy sex in a cold boat with a man who's a cross between Gerard Depardieu and the Incredible Hulk.

Eric bites my ear, pulls out another hairgrip with his teeth. I feel my hairstyle lurch. There's a ladder in my tights and being yanked to thigh level has done nothing for my pale linen shift dress.

I remember something. 'Eric, aren't you supposed to be giving your best man's speech round about now?'

Eric groans. 'Let's just stay here. Maybe they'll think I'm ill. God, I'm horny again. How did that happen? Is it the moon or something?'

'It's your brother's wedding.'

'Paul hates me.'

'He doesn't.'

'Well, I hate him.'

'Have you got the words in your pocket?'

'What words?'

'Don't tell me…' I sit up, even though Eric has started to draw circles around my nipple with the tips of his fingers and it feels divine. 'You haven't written a speech? You've known you were going to be your brother's best man for ten months and you haven't even planned what to say?'

In the ungenerous light from the thin sliver of moon, I see my husband's features assemble into a grin. He takes a long draw from the champagne bottle and bubbles trickle down his chin. 'You should lick that off. Good quality booze, this. Probably Sacha Distel used to drink it.'

'Come on, Eric. Your family'll never speak to us again if we cock this up. We're already on a yellow card for forgetting your dad's birthday, sending your cousin a 'congratulations on your baby boy' card when she had a girl, and not telling them we were going to India for three months last year…' I could go on. Eric's not so much the black sheep of his family as the Colonel Gadafy.

'How about a hand job, then? It won't take long, the size of the stiffy I've got.'

'Is that your mother?'

Sure enough, there at the entrance to the *salle des fetes*, is the shape of my mother-in-law, Julie. Her silhouette is spiky and triangular, hands on hips, feet slightly apart. In the dark we can only imagine the expression on her face. My money's on the tight-lipped disapproval that seems to be her default setting.

'The stiffy I *had*,' Eric mutters, as we plod out of the boat and make our way back to the Pavilion like school-children heading for detention.

Probably the best adjective to describe my mother-in-law is 'precise'. From her blonde hair that's swept into a much better upholstered arrangement than mine, to her neat, white shoes that, although having trudged from *mairie* to church to *vin d'honneur* to the reception will still be spotless, she's accurate, measured, perfectly planned and executed. When we're invited to dinner, which, thankfully for Eric's dad's blood pressure, isn't often, I feel like putting my hand up if I want to ask a question.

'Everyone's looking for you,' Julie says pointedly to Eric and I surmise the quick flicker of her eyes over my face means *but not you.* 'Where've you been?'

'Fucking. What does it look like?'

Julie's expression doesn't falter. 'Do you know you're supposed to be giving your speech? I wish you'd think about other people for a change. Where's your tie?'

'Shit! My tie? What happened to my gay tie?' Eric pushes the door to the *salle des fetes* as if it was a wild west saloon and he's here for a shooting.

'Wow! Time goes quickly,' I smile, but Julie's gone. I realise she's pressed a paper hankie into my hand, from which I suppose I'm to surmise that my mascara has run.

In the *salle des fetes*, Eric's on a roll. The guests sit around the gigantic U shape of the table, their faces turned to Eric standing between bride and groom at the top.

'And being best man for Paul…' Eric booms, a dreamy look in his eyes, 'feels like a *bridge*. On this side are the bad times – the fights we had as kids, the time I broke his arm, the times I beat him at chess.'

Everyone laughs. Paul looks mystified. I can tell this is the first he's heard of the chess.

'And on the other side, to which I'm crossing now, are the happier moments that I know we're about to embrace not only as *brothers*, but as *friends*. Walks in the countryside together, shared jokes, Sunday afternoons on his boat…'

Paul fiddles with his tie as if he's too hot. There's more chance of hell freezing over than his ever letting Eric near his boat.

'Sharing life's ups and downs together…' Eric continues.

Everyone goes 'ahhhh' and I notice most of the women have small smiles playing around their lips. At a rough estimate, sixty percent of them will be imagining him naked. I look at Julie, lips pursed, not believing a word. Her husband, Jean-Michel, rubs his chest like he's got heartburn.

'Because underneath it all,' Eric's still rolling, 'it's about *blood*. When you share blood, you can get through anything. That's why me and Paul, we're friends, *best* friends…'

Paul suddenly jumps up and starts to clap, obviously hoping to draw a line under the speech before things get even messier. They're so unlike each other, Eric and Paul, they don't even look as if they're from the same planet, let alone family. Paul is slim and compact, his hair a neatly trimmed halo of ash blond. He's had the same job in risk assessment for an insurance company since leaving school. Eric changes jobs like he changes shirts and probably thinks ‘risk assessment’ is the name of one of the bands they play on the late-night rock show he listens to.

Eric stoops to give Paul an enormous kiss on the cheek and Paul makes a big thing of patting Eric’s back in the way that body language experts always say means ‘under this display of bonhomie, I actually wish you’d fuck off’.

‘Oh, and another scenario I’ve just thought of…’ Eric booms. ‘I’m just thinking how nice it’ll be when Paul and Celine’s future children and our children, mine and Karen’s, play together…’

Eric looks at me and smiles. I don’t smile back. *Our children?* I feel I’ve just been thumped in the stomach.

‘What are you trying to tell us, Eric?’ shouts a tipsy voice.

‘Is it true?’ shouts someone else. ‘It is. It’s true, isn’t it? Congratulations, Karen!’

‘Sorry?’ A lock of hair falls into my eyes, pulling the rest of what remained of my hairstyle with it. Somewhere in the background I hear, ‘You didn’t tell us you were expecting, Eric! How long to go?’

A woman puts her hand on my stomach. ‘A boy,’ she proclaims. ‘Fifty years and I’ve never got it wrong.’

I lose track of all the congratulations that are coming my way. I see Eric at the head of the table, beaming like he’s just come out of the maternity ward and is holding the baby already.

‘If you’ll… excuse me…’ I hardly feel the doors as I swing through them.

That’s the good thing about being pregnant, I think, as I head into the ladies. You can get away with rushing off from a hundred people who are waiting to congratulate you, pat your stomach and talk about baby names, without anyone thinking it’s strange.

Only… I’m not pregnant.

And, I realise, as I look round and notice two huge steel sinks and a health and safety notice on the wall, neither am I in the ladies. I seem to be in one of the caterers’ kitchens. But at least here I’m not hearing congratulations.

‘Congratulations,’ says a voice. It’s one of the waiters, drying a champagne flute with a tea-towel. ‘I just heard when I was collecting the empties.’

‘Do me a favour,’ I say, ‘and don’t pat my stomach.’

‘I’ve always thought that’s impolite,’ he says, but gives my stomach a good look anyway. ‘So you’re … what? Three months gone? It hardly shows.’

'Funny, that.' I go for sarcasm even though it'll be lost on him.

'Anyway… can I help you?'

'Sorry?'

'You're in the kitchen. Did you want something?'

'Cigarette?'

'Is that wise in your condition?'

'There is no condition.' And there it is, out there, before I've had the chance to remember that this man is a stranger and my fertility is therefore of no concern to him. Oh well, in for a penny… 'It's fictional. My husband made it up.'

'Ah.'

By rights the waiter should be backing away now, leaving the bad-tempered English woman, her batty husband and fake pregnancy alone, but he's still there, rubbing the same glass. I wonder which is the better of the two options: facing the stranger, thinking I'm mad, or the whole of Eric's family, thinking I'm pregnant.

'My husband just got a bit ahead of himself,' I explain. 'We're trying for a baby, and…'

'Right.'

'Do you have children?' I look at him for the first time. He's as tall as Eric but much slimmer. His hair is dark brown and his features are neat and perfectly symmetrical. He's good-looking in a way that isn't sexy, like a man in a catalogue, modelling cardigans.

'Me?' His look wavers between alarmed and appalled. 'I *hate* children!'

Although it's inappropriate, I can't help a laugh.

1st Chapter of a Creative Non-Fiction Book: 1st Prize
Ursula Hurley

Heartwood

'He looks like a horse's arse, he smells like a horse's arse...' roared the rugby team as they charged around the quad. I tried to follow but I was laughing so hard I couldn't breathe. The lake of Dry Blackthorn between my head and my feet made walking difficult. Rakesh, the captain, scooped me up as he passed and set me aloft on his shoulders. 'Faster!' I yelled, kicking his sides. Fist in the air, I urged them on like some demented Boadicea. Rakesh tripped, pitching me towards the cobbled floor. Somehow he caught me and swung me up and around, whirling me until I was dizzy. I tipped back my head and looked at the sky, where the stars streamed as though they were on over-exposed film. Then he swung me low (sweet chariot) and laid me gently in an open dustbin. When he'd stopped laughing, he turned and walked away. We never spoke. When we were sober (which was, admittedly, not often) we ignored each other. I was his drinking buddy, the Absinthe fairy. Beyond that I did not exist.

'Come on,' said Mike, my Other Half, wedging his hands under my arms and hoisting me out of the bin.

'Good job it was empty,' I panted, dusting myself down.

'What shall we do now?' he asked, lighting a cigarette.

What I should have done now was go back to my room, make a large black coffee, and get on with my Shakespeare essay. But cider logic was in charge. 'Drink more, obviously.'

Mike offered his arm and we wove through Second Court, where the bar was calling last orders. As we wobbled over the shadowy cobbles of Third Court I looked up at Professor Rattigan's window but all was dark. My essay was due in tomorrow and I knew it was bad. I had to face it: the token Northerner from a bog-standard comprehensive simply couldn't cut it.

We stopped on the Bridge of Sighs so Mike could take a piss. 'Do you have to?' I asked, looking away in disapproval. Back home this was yobbery. Here it was high spirits.

''Fraid so,' he said. 'I couldn't wait.'

'Well I need to go too, but I bloody well *have* to wait, don't I?'

'Oh, I don't know,' said Mike, buttoning his jeans. 'I reckon we could rig up a funnel and a hose pipe down at the labs. I could make it my final year project.'

'I'm not holding your hand now,' I said over my shoulder as I walked on into New Court.

'Maybe Cat's having a party,' said Mike. 'Let's go and see.'

'OK,' I said uncertainly. Cat was rather like Holly Golightly, except she went somewhat more heavily. I wasn't sure if she was my friend, or just someone doing the same course who stopped for the occasional chat. To be honest, I was intimidated by her famous parents, her beauty and her wealth. I didn't want her to think of me as a hanger-on or an autograph chaser.

'Darling!' trilled Cat as she rose unsteadily from the table and teetered towards us. She gave Mike a lavish hug and a kiss on both cheeks. It may have been my imagination, but I thought she stiffened slightly when she saw me. If she did she disguised it winningly, hugging and kissing me too before returning to her seat, where she toyed with a leathery-looking fried egg on toast. She lit a cigarette, inhaled deeply, then said, 'Fuck it,' and stubbed it out in the egg. 'That's boarding school for you. I've been living on crisps and fags for so long I can't eat anything else. Still, it kept me out of the way while Mummy had her *glittering* career. What's a minor eating disorder compared to that?' She poured herself a large slug of gin and downed it in one, slamming the glass on the table.

She looked like she was going to cry, and I wondered whether I should try to comfort her. I was about to risk it when Mike lunged for the stereo. I jumped as *Cabaret* blared from the speakers.

'Come on old girl,' said Mike, rubbing her shoulder. 'Show must go on and all that. Knock off the gin, it never helps. Here,' he said, opening her drinks cabinet, 'let's make cocktails. Ursuls, you know how to make a Cosmo, don't you?'

'Erm,' I said. The only Cosmo I knew was a magazine.

Cat rested her head on Mike's chest and smiled as she closed her eyes. He stroked her hair fraternally. Then she jumped up. 'Cosmos ahoy! Get the vodka out of the freezer, will you?'

I hastened to comply, helping myself to a nip in the kitchen – the Dry Blackthorn had worn off, leaving me with the social skills of an amoeba.

Cat attempted something complicated with limes and triple sec, while Mike did a really bad impression of Tom Cruise in *Cocktail* (to whom he bore a passing resemblance and never let you forget it). I hung around like a spare part, noticing Cat's underwear spread to dry on the radiators. Expensive little scraps of silk and lace. A far cry from the ninety-nine pence polyester that covered my beanpole modesty.

Just then Razz burst in, closely pursued by Sebastian who was trying to stab him in the back with a large white mooli radish. They started mincing about to the music, and suddenly there was a party going on. 'Beedle dee, dee dee dee...' sang Razz, putting a pair of Cat's knickers on his head.

'Two ladies!' shouted Sebastian, as he tried to fasten one of Cat's bras over his t-shirt.

Mike settled down to roll a spliff and I, having downed two Cosmos, found that I suddenly had the talent and charisma of Liza Minnelli.

'Hush!' Everyone ignored Cat, so she tapped a glass as if she were making a speech. 'Oh,' she gasped, splitting her fishtail skirt as she clambered upon a table. Glasses crunched. A bottle of wine toppled.

That got Razz's attention. 'Spillage!' He sprinted over and slid on his knees as though he were racing a cricket ball to the boundary. He stopped beneath Cat and looked appreciatively up her skirt.

'*Dirty* Razz,' growled Sebastian.

Cat placed her stiletto heel on Razz's nose. He began to lick it.

'Darlings…' Cat persisted.

Sebastian turned the music off.

'Maybe this time, I'll be lucky... ' I yowled, spinning around to find everyone looking at Cat who was looking at me.

'Could you kill the vocals please, darling? I've got something important to say.'

'We've not run out of booze have we?' I asked, alarmed.

'Run out of grog? Don't be ridiculous darling!' Cat undulated like a charmed cobra.

'She's getting married,' wailed Razz, who prostrated himself in despair. When he realised that he had come to rest in a puddle of wine, he slurped contentedly.

Cat shot him a look which said 'if only'. Despite film-star looks her desperation seemed to repel all-comers. Then she smoothed down her skirt and said, 'I think there's someone knocking at the door.'

'Balls! It's the porter!' I ran to Mike, snatched the spliff from his fingers and threw it out of the open window. He didn't seem to notice.

Cat edged the heavy, studded oak door inwards. She had a cigarette in one hand and a cocktail in the other, so it was perhaps inevitable that she slopped half a Cosmopolitan down her cleavage as the door caught on a rug. 'Oh. Hello darling,' she said, patting ineffectually at her wet décolletage.

Razz grabbed the door and wrenched it open to reveal Nathan the Natski (Natural Scientist and all round anorak, never seen in the bar, and therefore a non-person to the drinking majority). Wisps of hair floated untidily over the dome of his already balding head. He was flushed, and his glasses awry.

'I'm trying to work,' he said grimly.

'Well don't! It's midnight on a Saturday. Come in and have a drink, darling.'

Nathan looked with distaste at Cat's gleaming wet bosom. 'We don't all have rich parents. Some of us have to make our own way. I need this degree. Just stop being so selfish, yeah?'

'*I* haven't got rich parents. Some of us can work *and* enjoy ourselves…' Anyone who didn't worship Bacchus inspired irrational fury in me. I suppose it was because I knew, deep down, that they were making something happen in their lives, while I was squandering my health and my money chasing this illusory euphoria.

Spurred on by guilt and fear I surged forward to continue the argument, but Nathan had disappeared up the spiral staircase.

'Jumped up little jism-monkey,' spat Sebastian.

'I'm not having this!' I snatched the mooli radish from him and lunged for the door.

I stomped up the stairs, heart pounding. Mike panted loudly behind.

We stood, swaying gently. Nathan's outer door was closed, which meant that he most definitely did not wish to be disturbed.

I banged on the door anyway.

'Erm, I don't think he'll come out,' ventured Mike.

'Why not?' I asked.

'Would *you* want to come out and talk to you?' He grinned unconvincingly. 'Look.' Mike pointed to a small, arched door. It was about five feet tall, made of wood and painted grey. It hugged the curve of the staircase. An inch of shadow indicated that the door was not properly closed. Cold seemed to leach through the gap.

'Ay, that's never been open before. Where does it go?' I asked.

'Tottenham Court Road,' said Mike gravely.

'Piss off,' I snarled.

'Well how should I know?' Mike's tone was slightly apologetic.

'You know everything. You went to public school.'

Mike turned the ring which raised the latch. The door swung open on well-oiled hinges. There was a smell of old dust.

'Are we allowed?'

'I can't see a No Entry sign.' Mike ducked and stepped inside. I followed. We crouched as we shuffled through a cramped passageway, and found ourselves on the lead flashings next to a gargoyle.

'Wow.' There was a gentle wind up here, which caught my hair and snagged it in my lip gloss.

We peered out over the Backs; a huge expanse of blackness which covered trees and water and ornamental lawns. A moorhen spiked the darkness with a disembodied cackle. Far away occasional street lights glowed weakly. It could have been the vodka, but looking up at the sky gave me the sensation of peering down into a bottomless well.

Mike sat on a ridge tile and lit a cigarette. The tip burned fiercely in the fresh air. It seemed to trace scarlet lines across my retinas. I sat next to him, my tights offering little protection from the cold rough stone. The Cosmos wore off and I began to shiver. Mike put his arm around me. He had on a checked Timberland shirt and I could feel the warmth of his flesh through it.

'Aren't you cold?' I asked him.

'I don't feel it.'

We sat a while in silence. Mike flicked his cigarette stub out into the darkness. I nestled into his shoulder.

'Shooting star,' said Mike.

'Where?' He pointed and I followed the line of his arm, but I saw only fixed dots of light. I didn't let on.

'You're supposed to make a wish,' said Mike.

'OK.' I wondered what I would wish for, if my fairy godmother existed.

'It won't come true unless you say it out loud,' persisted Mike.

I got the feeling that he was prodding me in a particular direction, but I didn't have a clue what he wanted me to say. So I told the truth. 'I wish I'd never started this degree.'

'Oh.' Mike lit another cigarette and inhaled deeply. He turned away. His jaw muscles bulged. 'By extension that means you wish we'd never met.'

'No!' Oh crap, I'd really put my foot in it now. 'I didn't mean that. Of course I don't wish that we'd never met. It's just that this degree has caused so much hassle. I've fallen out with my family, I'm clearly a thorn in the side of the tutors here, and I'd rather pull my own teeth out than sit through another seminar where I'm made to feel like a complete moron.' I realised that I was on the verge of tears. 'I'm probably going to fail. If it wasn't for you I would have dropped out last year.'

'So it's nothing personal, then?' asked Mike.

I smiled up at him and he brushed my cheek with a tobacco-scented finger.

'I could have a solution,' he said, fiddling with his Zippo. If I didn't know better I'd swear he was nervous. I'd never seen him so twitchy.

'I love you,' he blurted. Bloody hell! He'd said the 'L' word. Unprompted. This was massive.

'I love you, too.' Inside I was beaming. He'd said it first! What a coup!

'Yeah,' he said, returning to flippancy, 'U2 are a really good band.'

I rolled my eyes. 'Don't be childish.'

'Why not?' he asked, eyes shining. 'I love being childish. I love children. And I'd like to have them with you.'

At the mention of children my heart began to thud. I hadn't expected this so soon. I thought I had a little longer to find a way of telling him. My jaw was locked. I couldn't speak.

Mike knelt down and took my hand. 'That's why I'm asking you to marry me.' Before I knew what had happened, he'd slipped a gold ring on my engagement finger. But...

'Aren't we a bit young?' I asked. 'I mean, are you sure this is what you want? There's no rush, is there?'

'I'm totally certain. Not only do I want to spend the rest of my life with you, but I think I've found a way to take the pressure off. When Mum married Dad she got a job in the family firm. There's a job waiting for me when I graduate, and if we're married then they'll find you a job too. It might be a PA or something at first, but it means you can tell Rattigan to shove Shakespeare where the sun don't shine.'

I gaped. 'I don't know what to say.'

'How about 'yes'? Think about it: we get to be together. No money worries. I'll end up in a senior position – I've got to, I'm the boss's son. And when you want to stop and have children... well, whenever you're ready. How many do you want, by the way?'

Tell him, said the voice in my head. *Tell him now, before this goes any further. Give him the chance to walk away.* 'Erm, I've never really thought about it.' I was a coward. I was selfish and deceitful and someday my lack of candour would come back and bite me on the arse.

'Are you OK?' asked Mike. 'You look pale.'

'Erm, yeah,' I lied, 'I'm just overwhelmed.'

He cradled the back of my head in his hand, tangling his fingers in my hair as he drew me to him.

Some time later we decided to leave the stars to their own devices. Mike stopped in the narrow passageway. 'Hmmm.'

'What?'

'Door won't open.' He took out his Zippo and flicked the flame into life. The smell of lighter fuel was strong in the small space. Curved masonry and wavering cobwebs snapped into view. 'Someone's locked it. You'll have to shout for help.'

'Me?'

'I'm too embarrassed,' said Mike.

I pushed past him and shoved the door. I kicked it hard. The wood shivered but didn't move. 'Bollocks.'

'Yes, two.'

'Very funny.' I put my shoulder to it and barged. 'Ow!'

'I'm going to see if I can get a message to Cat,' said Mike, turning away.

'How are you going to do that?'

'Throw something down at her window.' Mike went back outside and started looking for missiles. There was a sharp sound, like someone had cracked a giant egg, and Mike swore loudly.

'Bloody engineers,' I muttered. 'Hello? Can anyone hear me? We're locked on the roof!'

Eventually, the door swung open. In the bright yellow arch of electric light, Natski Nathan was silhouetted.

'I'm so sorry for disturbing you again…' I blustered, hating the role of groveller.

'You're lucky I was passing – I was just going down to the Porters' Lodge to report a smashed window.'

'Oh,' I gasped, rather too theatrically, 'perhaps a bird hit it.'

'A bird *brain*, more like,' said Nathan.

'Oh dear,' I faltered, 'do you think someone...'

'A roof tile. Quite deliberate. Upper class yobbery if you ask me.' Nathan was tight-lipped with anger, and I shifted uneasily from one foot to the other, hoping that Mike could hear this conversation and had the sense to keep out of the way until I'd managed to get us off the hook.

I smiled nervously and rubbed my arms to diffuse the goose bumps.

'You look cold,' said Nathan, softening. 'Would you like to come in for a coffee?'

'Erm… thanks, that's really kind…'

'Nice one, Ursuls!' Mike emerged and put his arms around my waist.

'Say thank you to Nathan, he's just let us out.' I looked meaningfully at Mike, but he ignored me.

'Ta very much,' he called over his shoulder as he started his descent to the party.

I turned to thank Nathan again.

'I think this belongs to you.' He shoved the mooli into my hand and slammed his door.

Poetry: 1st Prize
Annisa Suliman

Ice etching

my eyes
skating on ice
glide over you
ethereal in blue morning haze
Gauloise in hand
head against the window pane

a black tarry smell explores the room
telling tales of French Revolution
bloody streets
empty cells
staggering broken violet plumes
around your volatile self

my eyes
silent picture taking
click to etch the final frame
you
the door
the chair
Mayakovsky
The Clash
Picasso in slanted shade
Kerouac
Eliot
Conrad
barely there
stripped down bed
bagged guitar

every thing is out of time
out of place

Short Story: 2nd Prize
Peter Jordan

Death and the Boy

When I received the news that I was going to die, I was, quite simply, devastated. What is more, that I should be told on my birthday was a grim irony that only the grimmest of reapers would have found amusing. The day had begun so well too. It was a warm May morning. I sat facing the rest of the school holding a crinkly piece of shaped tin foil containing seven Smarties. One for each year. Smirking uncontrollably, I listened while my colleagues laboured through a rendition of the popular Christmas carol, *While Shepherds Watched Their Flocks By Night*. It was the policy of the school that birthday boys and girls were allowed to choose the hymn for assembly, on their special day. I had given the matter much careful thought before coming to my decision. The seasonal unsuitability of it had not occurred to me, but an alternative version of the carol that began, *While Shepherds Washed Their Socks By Night*, had. Looking at my classmates now, I was sure I could see one or two opting for this alternative version. The two very naughty Nigels had definitely washed their socks, otherwise they would not have been giggling quite so much.

I felt a great and incomprehensible surge of power as I sat there beaming from ear to ear. With a determined lust for life I crunched down on my last Smartie and wondered what other dizzying heights of achievement awaited me in the days, months and years to come.

But, sadly, my moment of glory was destined to evaporate before the end of that leafy innocent spring day. I was about to discover that I – just like everyone else on our benighted planet – was marked for extinction. Even finding out the previous year that Santa Claus did not exist paled before this unforeseen threat to a generally enjoyable, carefree and fulfilling life.

In retrospect, the Santa episode was obviously a dark presage of things to come. After a heated argument in painting class with my friend – at least I had thought he was my friend – Gary Babbs, I went home and reported to my mother that Gary was an atheist when it came to belief in Father Christmas. I fully expected her to call Mrs Babbs and denounce Gary as a dangerous free-thinker.

Having never seen my mother look sheepish before, I did not immediately recognise the odd expression on her face. It was not until she spoke that I realised the full extent to which I had been deceived by my own flesh and blood, my progenitor, my mother. How does one deal with a betrayal of such magnitude? There was still another week of school before the holiday. I was going to have to face Gary, knowing that I had been tricked into believing something as utterly implausible as a fat old man covering the surface of the entire world in the space of one night and leaving gifts for every child alive. How could I have been so stupid?

'Then who does fill my stocking?' I had demanded. Again, that sheepish look. This time I recognised it for what it was.

'Either me or your father.' Pathetic. Truly, pathetic. And why? Why did they think it appropriate to perpetrate such an appalling deception on their naively trusting son? What was the point of creating such an elaborate and, frankly, ridiculous myth? Who stood to gain from it?

Up till then, I had believed my parents were honest people, people who protected and nurtured me, people I could trust. What a ghastly, miserable nightmare to realise that Gary Babbs was more reliable than they were.

It had been difficult to adapt to these changed circumstances, but not half as difficult as it was to adapt to the fact that I was going to die at some point.

I found out about my ineluctable demise during what appeared at the time to be a perfectly innocent conversation, but then the Santa incident had also sprung from just such a seemingly innocuous origin. So, perhaps I should have known better.

I ran home at the end of the day, still brimming with pride and joy at my advanced years. There would be no party until the weekend, but there was a special tea. This included a cake covered with tiny silver balls as hard and unyielding as ball bearings, which gave my young teeth one of their first major challenges. The cake's soft smooth cream and jam sponge interior was somewhat compromised by these peculiarly resistant baubles. Yet neither this nor the fact that my mother's gift of a new suit of armour was clearly designed for a smaller and more compact child than I would ever be, could deflect my good humour. I sportingly squeezed into the plastic breastplate and wedged the helmet onto my head as best I could, although, try as I certainly did, the visor would not descend lower than the bridge of my nose.

Being a polite child, I did not immediately tear it and the breastplate off, even though they both pinched painfully in several places. I even managed a little half-hearted jousting with the sofa cushions – much to my mother's delight – before settling down to another portion of jelly and ice cream. Then, spurred on by my recently acquired mathematical prowess, I began telling my mother about what I planned to be doing when I was one hundred years old, and what I would hope to have achieved by age two hundred. I was about to go on to outline my plans for my three hundredth birthday, when my mother intervened. She pointed out that actually nobody had lived to be three hundred, or even two hundred for that matter, with the clear implication that I was not going to buck the prevailing trend. I was astounded. What on earth did she mean?

I should point out that I had already known for some time that life could end, but I thought it only happened by someone else's agency or by accident. I had therefore assumed that if you stayed out of trouble, you need not die at all, especially as there were no tyrannosauruses or velociraptors roaming around any more, at least not where I lived. Now, apparently, no matter how good a boy I was, I would still end up biting the dust along with Jesse James, Billy the Kid and any other two-bit outlaw. The idea obsessed me. More than that, it gripped my mind like a steel vice, offering no possibility of lateral thought whatsoever, because now it included *me*. It wasn't just something that happened to other people. It was personal.

Then the still unresolved Granny issue came to mind. Granny had 'passed away' a month or so before, and at the time, my mother had made it seem like a mystical and very special event in which Granny had floated – despite her considerable bulk – up into the sky. I think she must have noticed my sceptical look. A far more likely scenario as far as I was concerned was that she had been shot by bandits and wandered off wounded somewhere, maybe to protect us, although it didn't really seem in Granny's gift to be quite so heroic and unselfish. I couldn't make a lot of sense of 'passed'. Passed what? But 'away' was clear enough. Granny was away and was unlikely to come back. That suited me fine. Granny was a miserable old bat at the best of times. She was constantly reading books without pictures and moaning whenever I did anything except sit still and not speak. She did not like running around and making a noise, so there was really not a lot we had in common.

In the last few weeks before she 'passed away', she took to staring into space and ignoring me completely. So I did likewise. Two could play at that little game. In fact, it occurred to me at the time that Granny might just have upped sticks because she realised that I was more than a match for her. But now, it seemed that something altogether more sinister was afoot.

I pressed my mother as to when this event – this death – was going to happen. She said she didn't know. She said that no one knew when they were going to die. This from the person who had spent years pretending to be the fount of all wisdom? I didn't know whether to laugh or to cry.

'So when does it *usually* happen?' I asked, with what I felt was remarkable patience, all things considered.

'Oh not for a long time yet,' she said. 'After all, Granny was very old.'

'So Granny is dead is she? She hasn't just 'passed away' like you said, has she?' My mother must have realised she had just boxed herself into a very tight little corner. There was a silence, which I took to be evidence of maternal contrition. To be honest, I was slightly disappointed that it had not after all been the sheer charismatic power of my personality which had removed Granny from the scene. I broke the tension with a weary sigh.

'So how old was Granny?'

'Seventy-six.' I paused to calculate. According to my seven times table, that was very nearly eleven times my own age.

'What happens when I'm dead?'

'You'll go to Heaven.'

'Heaven?'

'Yes.'

'How will I get to… Heaven?'

'By being good.' I could see where this was leading and headed her off at the pass.

'And is that where Granny is?'

'Yes.'

Clearly the benchmark qualification for the Celestial City had been set pretty low, if bad-tempered moaning grannies could get there so easily.

'How do you know she's in Heaven? Did you drive her there?'

'Not exactly,' my mother said vaguely, completely missing my sardonic tone. I sighed again.

'OK. Let's begin at the beginning,' I said, imitating my father's usual opening gambit when interrogating me about a suspected misdemeanour. 'Where did Granny die?'

'In hospital.'

'And you just left her there?'

'No, no, of course not.'

'Well, what did you do with her then?' I think my mother could sense that the trap was closing around her.

'Well,' she said hesitantly, 'we buried her.'

'What?' I was horrified. The only time I had been buried was when my older brother and his friends had dug a pit for me at the beach. After coaxing me in with smiles and promises of great fun to be had, they held me down and shovelled sand into the hole until only my head protruded. Then they ran off laughing, while I screamed in terror until I breathed in some sand and had a coughing fit.

'Now listen,' said my mother, 'your father will be home in a minute and you need to have a bath. Off you go now. No more nonsense, young feller-me-lad.'

Nonsense? She could talk. What about her pack of lies about roly-poly red-nosed Santa and his workshop staffed by kindly little elves, and reindeers with silly names like Dasher and Prancer? The memory of Gary's gloating face when I had gone back to school the next day still made me sick to the stomach. Word of my astonishing gullibility spread like wildfire. Kevin Wickstead, Patrick Duffy and the two Nigels all had a whale of a time at my expense, although I was pretty sure they had been believers at some point. The difference was that they had not been drawn into an argument and forced to defend this fundamental tenet of Christmas faith.

The nadir of my humiliation had come when Marianne Fishnor decided I was persona no longer grata. Our budding romance was well and truly nipped for all time. There were no more secret smiles. No more sharing her chocolate and letting me bite where she had bitten. No more handstands in the playground. I would never get to see her Confederate grey knickers ever again.

I was alone. Totally alone. And now... only the grave beckoned.

Seventy-six years. That was an awfully long time. Impossible to imagine really. As impossible to imagine as the stretch of time between us and when dinosaurs were fighting and eating each other. But it would happen. Eventually. And I had an uncomfortable inkling what it might be like.

Once, when playing Cowboys and Indians with my brother and his friends, my character, a loyal Native American guide called Running Antelope, had been shot in an unequal firefight. As a consolation, I was allowed to loose one final arrow into the air, which they assured me was a very noble gesture that would always be remembered by them; that is, by their gun-slinging alter egos. I was momentarily convinced by this argument and seduced by the attention I received in the short-term, but I soon realised the unbearable boredom of being dead. Basically, I could either watch them continue their adventure – and it did not escape my notice that far from taking the memory of Running Antelope to their hearts, my name was never mentioned again – or I could go and do something else by myself. Some choice. Like having to choose between the electric chair and lethal injection, or between gassing and hanging.

Of course, I knew plenty about executions. It was one of my brother's favourite topics. He told me that history was all about people getting their heads chopped off, or being burnt at the stake, or once in a while being subjected to that mysterious process of being hanged, drawn and quartered. Staying alive while you expired slowly and violently. I always thought it was a better option than being beheaded, because you had that much more time to live. The idea of extreme pain did not seem to feature in these deliberations. Nor did I ponder how one could fruitfully use those extra minutes of life, while your innards were pulled out and burned in front of your eyes.

I had dawdled for as long as I could on my way to the bathroom. Then just as I reached the door, I remembered that I felt a little peckish. I veered away and headed for the fridge, where I helped myself to a small section of treacle tart. Not my favourite. But it filled a hole, or rather, a void.

After the eternity of bathtime, I found myself once more in pyjamas and having my toenails cut. Bedtime was approaching. Death seemed to be miles away, and as my mother lay my head on her lap and began twirling a cotton bud in my ear, I felt a kind of ecstasy. My father was listening to some music and staring into space. My mother was trying to talk to him. Like with all adult conversations, I filtered out the words that did not interest me and all those I did not understand. I was left with, 'today, school, boy, death, Granny, Heaven'. My father chuckled and said, rather mysteriously I thought, that he was listening to Sherbet's death and the maiden... Even sherbet was ultimately doomed... I drifted off for a brief timeless minute, before being gently shaken back to life.

'Hey, wake up mister. Time to turn in. Shadrach, Meshach, and Abednego!' My mother tipped me off her lap and I wandered away. 'Daddy will come and read you a story in a minute,' she called after me.

Sliding between the cool sheets, I waited for the family patriarch to turn up. I knew that before story time, there would be the ritual enquiry, 'What have you learned today?' I wondered whether I had the nerve to tell him what was in my heart. That grown-ups were even better and more prolific fibbers than children like me could ever be. That I would trust nothing and nobody ever again. That sceptical, even cynical, detachment was the only valid stance for a thinking being to adopt.

There was a side light on. It threw my recumbent shadow onto the wall. I raised my hand and saw its enlarged outline do likewise. Making a flat, closed palm – as if about to do a karate chop – then raising my thumb toward the ceiling and moving my little finger down and up, I made a passable impression of a horse opening and shutting its mouth. Gary Babbs had shown me how to do this. I felt depressed. Gary seemed to be ahead of me in everything.

I should have been more grateful. Gary was the first of many distractions which helped me to ignore – for a long time yet – the endless, soundless, unblinking, peek-a-boo dark that was already gaping vacuously at me through a chink in the curtains.

Creative Non-Fiction Essay: 2nd Prize
William Prince

A Writhing Mass

Okell arrived today. A big box from America: *Burmese: An Introduction to the Spoken Language* and *Burmese: An Introduction to the Script.* 700 pages and fourteen cassettes. Is this feasible, I wonder?

Since Okell leaves me the choice, I'm going to start with the script. Sound, meaning and spelling form a triangle; if one side is missing, the other two are suspended in empty space. It's possible, of course, to learn to speak without reading but what you lose is not just one side of the triangle, but the pleasure of deciphering street signs, menus and other essential props of daily life. Furthermore, as Okell points out, Roman script is inadequate to convey pronunciation: Burmese has too many sounds that simply don't exist in English.

Linguists call it 'focus on form': my brain will identify letters, link them to sounds and I shall be able to read. It did that with English – once upon a time. Surely it can do it again? As I open the book to lesson one, I can feel the neurons crackle with excitement.

Form-focused learners are patient, meticulous, they like to get things right. They think before they speak, then come out with something like: 'Had she been made aware of the consequences of her decision, she would have been less delighted than she was.' Not an easy comment to place in a conversation but form-focused learners are more concerned with shapely syntax than nattering with the neighbours; they're happy enough to speak to the mirror and provide the answer themselves: 'Though her not being made aware may have been regrettable, her delight was a joy to behold.'

I doubt if I'll ever produce such gems, but who knows? This is the start of a long, exotic journey, and for the moment, in any case, I have no one to speak to.

Why am I learning Burmese? Because I don't know it. A challenge. For much of my life I've taught English in France, explained to trainee teachers how it's done, studied second language acquisition. But how long is it since I learnt a language myself? I'd have to go back 30 years. Time to remedy that, I thought, and while I'm at it, I might as well be ambitious. Not for me the same old boring 26 letters as in

English. What would that prove? Does a pole-vaulter set the bar at two metres?

Burmese letters have none of our alphabet's spikiness. They're a soft succession of loops and curves, legacy of the times when texts were scratched onto palm leaves with a metal stylus – straight lines were avoided as they tended to rip the leaf. According to Okell, the script has 33 consonants, 'some eight vowels' and no capitals. A few pages later he says of the vowels that traditionally there are twelve, so there seems to be a little uncertainty here. Either way, he sweetens the pill by pointing out that English has 26 capitals on top of the lower case letters – a greater learning load than Burmese. I'm dubious. Are O and V really different from o and v? The same could be said of practically half the alphabet. But I understand what he's trying to tell me – this is within your grasp. 'Don't despair,' he adds. 'Persevere. At first you see nothing but a writhing mass of symbols, but there comes a time when you wonder why it was difficult.' Hmm. Is that supposed to be encouraging?

It starts off well. Motivation is high, the neurons fizz and Okell has a pleasant, purring voice as he reads the instructions. The first few letters are distinctive, and matching them to sounds is like putting names to faces: cauliflower nose = Gerald, upturned eyebrows = Mandy. But it isn't long before I come across quadruplets: see them together and yes, there are features which allow me to tell them apart. But then when I meet just one of them, I confidently say, 'Hi, John,' only to be told, 'No, James, actually. But don't worry, persevere!' Oh, yes? With several sets of twins and triplets too? And now look – a fifth one! Quintuplets! Sextuplets! Aaargh…! At times I lose sight of the few distinctive features I've identified and mix up letters that don't even look alike. My form-focused neurons start to ache and groan. Ah, foolish pride! Grappling now with lesson eight, I see that I should have gone for a metre and a half.

But I persevere because there's another reason. I'm in love. A single week 33 years ago and I've been in love ever since. There are many reasons for falling in love with a country: climate, scenery, atmosphere, food – yes, there was that, but above all there were the people. The welcome they extend, their unfailing kindness and warmth, their quiet, patient strength in the face of adversity. By the time I left, Burma had worked its magic on me.

I would have preferred it to be just a crush, something I'd get over as soon as I went somewhere else. Like – what was her name? Daisy? Worked in the grocery store when my voice was starting to break. Those Tate and Lyle moments: I'd go in to buy a pack of lard and her voice and eyes would turn it to golden syrup. But she moved away and I moved on and now she's just a blur.

If only it could have been that way with Burma. I had no camera and the memories are disconnected fragments. I can look at each one, see a hint of the beauty, but what holds them together is lost, like the missing parts of an archaeologist's vase. But the spell that was cast has never worn off – the sweetness of that week is with me still. Enchanted for life.

If anything has moved, it's Burma. Back then it was run by General Ne Win, inventor of 'the Burmese path to socialism'. But although he firmly set up a dictatorship, ruined the economy, and sidled up to the infamous Khmer Rouge, he was still a bit of a softie compared to the current crop. They do have names but seem to prefer the ominously faceless 'the generals'. They changed the name of the country to Myanmar (dissidents make a point of sticking to 'Burma') and in the middle of nowhere built a new capital, to which they retreated, the better to rule, paranoid, xenophobic and vicious.

Which is why, approaching lesson twelve, 'You can't,' I said to myself. 'Don't you know what they're like? Torture, forced labour, child soldiers, systematic rape as a weapon of ethnic oppression – I could go on. But listen: 'Burma will be here for many years, so tell your friends to visit us later. Visiting now is tantamount to condoning the regime.' That's not me, it's Aung San Suu Kyi. How can you even be thinking of this? Boycott.'

I sigh with impatience. Of course I know what they're like. I don't need lectures like this. Who do I think I am? So damned righteous and smug! 'Give me a break. Who's talking about going there? I'm just learning the language, OK?'

'With no one to speak it to? *Oh, no, it's just for the challenge.* Huh! Who are you trying to kid? All that form-focussed guff. What about the motivation?'

OK, so I have a point. Motivation, yes, the key to it all. And it's true I've never been thrilled by present participles and auxiliaries. But that's always been my problem – too meaning-focused, too eager to chat, to bother with getting it right. Take my attempt at Spanish – pitiful. Yes, I could rattle away when I'd had enough Rioja, but was I saying anything intelligible? Because the grammar – well, imagine a farmer ploughing a field, who, instead of going up and down does a bit in the middle, a dozen yards down the side, a squiggle or two in the corner, and then thinks, 'Sod it, let's go and milk the cows.' There wouldn't be much to thank the Lord for when it comes to Harvest Festival.

Russian was even worse. That was back in the early 90s, when I cycled once a week to evening classes. Irina, the teacher, liked and respected her mother tongue; hearing it mangled caused her to wince in pain. Russian is full of inflectional morphology – the endings to words that indicate things like gender, number and whether the word is preceded by 'to' or 'of'. To me they were like glass jewellery, jangling and shimmering and generally getting in the way. I adopted a two-step approach: the word itself first, the bangles and beads can come later. But leaving out the morphology was equivalent to saying, 'Look, Irina, I know you think they're pretty, but can't you get rid of all those ablatives and datives? You'll look much better, you know.'

Irina didn't see it that way. After a while she stopped acknowledging my presence, calling instead upon my classmates, who, not being teachers themselves, were more obedient. 'My brother speaks Russian but my parents don't speak Chinese,' they could say in somewhat hesitant but perfectly inflected Russian, while I muttered along with them, impatient all the while to have an uninflected chat about the collapse of the Soviet Union.

Irina was right, of course. I myself have suffered many times at the hands – or the tongue – of over-enthusiastic, meaning-focused speakers, keen to improve their English. 'Thatcher no like miner, eh? Think you? Aw! Aw! What woman! She have ball, tell so!' No matter how sympathetic one is to the communicative approach, oral production of this sort is on a par with halitosis. How you react will depend on where you are. If you're in what applied linguists call a 'naturalistic setting' (more commonly known as a pub), your best bet is a naturalistic answer: 'Don't know what it is of yours she doesn't like, mate, but she's more on the ball than you are.' This should be delivered with a friendly smile, as if it's a perfectly coherent response which, given the speaker's level of proficiency, you are sure he will understand. When he looks bewildered – 'Repeat, please?' – you have your chance to pat him on the shoulder, say, 'Better luck next time,' and walk away.

As a teacher in a formal setting (the classroom), you can't get away so easily. 'Well done, François! Good try! But what do we need? Thatcher...? Thatcher...? An auxiliary? You know? She doesn't. She doesn't like. And an 's' perhaps? The miners. Thatcher doesn't like the miners. Can you repeat?'

But meaning-focused learners are oblivious to correction. 'Aw! Aw! What ball she have! But she good for you, yes, yes. You Britain like woman have ball! Aw! Aw!'

'Right, François, thank you very much. Now, let's get back to our original topic. Likes and dislikes. Marie, do you –'

'In France no possible woman be –'

'Marie, do you like shopping?'

It's a stupid question. A single glance at Marie is enough to tell you that she lives for *le shopping*, but this is not about real communication. 'Yes, I do. I like very much the shopping.'

'Ah, thank you, Marie. What a wonderful auxiliary. Yes, I do. But the article, no – ok?' Etcetera until you glance at your watch. 'My goodness, how time flies!'

'Eh, no! It still have five minute!'

'I think your watch must be slow, François. Right, have a good evening, everyone. See you next week!'

So yes, I do sympathise with Irina. But she cut me out with such deep permafrost that I quit. Ah, that motivation. Get ignored by your teacher for a few sloppy accusatives or mislaid genitives and it's punctured.

Meanwhile, I've been stuck on lesson twenty for a month. In fact the last time I opened the book, the symbols seethed so wildly that I had to slam it shut before they wriggled off the page. It was the stacked consonants that did it. The killed consonants were fine, and so was the rider on the forehead. I even managed the three different tones, high, low and creaky (though it sounds more like a croak than a creak to me). But then along came the stacked consonants and my brain cells went on strike. 'Right lads, hold up a sec! Time for a vote. See that up ahead? Pain barrier. Hands up who's ready to go through it. Right. Thought as much. We're all agreed then. Focus on form? Sorry, guv, the lads ain't having it!'

Well, who can blame them? All that time getting used to shapes that follow each other like a docile flock behind Little Bo Peep, then all of a sudden they start to play piggy back. Not only that, but in order to fit on the palm leaf, they're chopped a bit here and squashed a bit there, till they no longer sashay across the page but hobble around like hunchback amputees. My frazzled neurons are downing tools in droves. My motivation has sprung a serious leak.

So I have an idea. What if I go there after all? I'll never manage otherwise. Just a quick trip this August. I'll read the shop signs, practise my creaky tones and be out before my sanctimonious other self even notices. And I'll be *responsible*, you know? That's what they say at *Lonely Planet* – you don't have to stay in government hotels or journey by MTT (Myanmar Travel and Tours, whose profits end up in the pockets of the generals). With a minimum of care, you can make sure your money goes to private individuals. And you're not just giving them money – that's not what they're after, it's simply what they need – but a chance to meet someone from the outside world, who just for a moment can free them from isolation.

'You seriously want to go through with this?' I've talked it over with my wife, who's up for it, and I'm fixing dates and looking at flights when the voice calls down again, scathing, outraged, from the moral high ground. 'I know I'm annoying you, but since you refuse to listen, what else can I do? Let me give you another quote. "Burmese people know their own problems better than anyone else. They know what they want – they want democracy – and many have died for it. To suggest that there's anything new that tourists can teach the people of Burma about their own situation is not simply patronising – it's also racist." By the way, you know they've prolonged her house arrest?'

'Some retard American swam to her house and they used that as an excuse. Yes, I know. So when they hold their so-called elections, there'll hardly even be an opposition. Yes,' I say wearily, 'but look, the Democratic Voice of Burma carries an article saying tourism should be encouraged. Not just to break the isolation, but get this – the more tourists there are, the more the regime has to monitor what they get up to, which drains their resources, so the more space there is for political dissidents to operate in.' I sit back smiling, barely able to suppress my glee. I mean, how's that for cunning?

But always there comes a rejoinder: how could that happen when the regime has infiltrated every level of society and you can't be sure that even your private guesthouse isn't being forced to pay a kickback to the government? We're not talking mild oppression here.

Burma is up there with North Korea and Zimbabwe. What we're talking here is the Burmese path to *Nineteen Eighty-Four*.

And so the debate goes on, my two selves refusing to budge, until one morning the matter is settled by outside intervention: a message from my nephew inviting us to his wedding. In August. In Vancouver.

Well, maybe it's all for the best. We'll spend our holidays and cash in democratic, tolerant, freedom-loving Canada. There'll be no spies, no guilt, no sensitive topics to avoid. But the part of me that's quietly smirking in triumph knows that it hasn't won yet. So it won't be this year? No matter. I can wait.

There's no point denying it: love is irrational and selfish, it will try every trick in the book. There's every reason to boycott, yes, I admit. But once you've got Burma under your skin, you're not going to meekly stay away, even if begged to by Aung San Suu Kyi herself. Focus on form, learn a new language as a challenge – why, that was just a sly manoeuvre to justify buying the books. I'm not a form-focused learner and I never have been. And now that my true motives are unmasked, I can turn to *Burmese: An Introduction to the Spoken Language*. No more wrestling with symbols that won't stay still – this is all about words that relate to the world. Because listen to something else I've found: south of Bagan, in the village of Yenan-Gyaung, the director of an orphanage is calling for volunteers to teach the children English. Now *there's* responsible tourism, surely?

Lesson one: *museum, pagoda, park, hotel, market*. My meaning-focused neurons leap into action. The motivation is back.

'Hah! We'll soon see how long it lasts. Help in an orphanage? Very convenient – your conscience washed whiter than white! Did you read, by the way, about the generals' plans to build a nuclear weapon?'

Oh, Okell, if only you knew what a writhing mass of contradictions you've let loose.

For further information:
www.voicesforburma.org – NGO devoted to responsible tourism in Burma.
www.dvb.no – The Democratic Voice of Burma, run by Burmese exiles based in Oslo, provides impartial news and analysis.
www.burmacampaign.org.uk – Campaigns for democracy and human rights in Burma and urges tourists to boycott.

Flash Fiction: 2nd Prize
Phillip Sheahan

The Tattooist

When the bell on the door of the shop rattled the tattooist rarely looked to see who had entered. The gallery of Gothic themes and mystical creatures was enough to prompt most casual visitors to beat a hasty retreat. Those who did not hurry away faced a second test. The tattooist's face. Another work of art: a tribute to the art of the plastic surgeon. To this 'art work' the tattooist had added two words – 'for valour', written so small that one needed to lean close to read them. Few were that brave. Or that curious. Who cares to know the true price of a Victoria Cross?

The woman with the alabaster skin and long dark hair who entered the tattooist's shop that morning did not recoil at the sight of his grotesque display. She looked about her with a face that beamed confidence and joy. The tattooist noted that she seemed to sniff the air as an animal might do.

'Can I help you?' he said when he could stay his curiosity no longer.

'I'd like a tattoo. The most beautiful thing you have ever seen or ever imagined. And I want it where only my lover will see it.'

The tattooist had never heard a request expressed with such clarity and purpose.

'Look around you,' he said. 'I am not the artist for you. My work is too dark.'

'I am not afraid of darkness. What is felt and understood by the heart is all that matters. Here I sense poetry and adventure. That is enough.'

'And your lover, has he no say in the matter?'

'I have no lover. But I live with hope. Do we have an agreement?'

'On one condition,' said the tattooist. 'That what I create remains my secret. I will never reveal or describe it to you but leave that pleasure to your lover. I promise only that it will be, as you request, the most beautiful thing I have ever seen or imagined.'

The tattooist was true to his word and only on her wedding night did her lover describe in detail the miniature portrait of the girl with alabaster skin and flowing hair tattooed on her back. Her eyes would never see it, but her heart would know its beauty through the words and the caresses of her lover, the tattooist, in whose voice she found poetry, adventure and valour.

1st Chapter of a Novel: 2nd Prize
Malcolm Bray

The Resurrection of Danny MacNamara

Just like the flowers I'm gonna grow wild, I got no mamma's kisses, no daddy's smile (*Nobody's Child*, Cy Coben)

Julia Jane Foster was sixteen when she met Donald. First generation Irish catholic, she was not the sort of girl to do anything foolish. But she went right ahead and broke that mould with Don. No hesitation. Whether it was his rugged charm, the black wavy hair or the '68 Mustang, the outcome was a quick-fix marriage at Salome's Hitch 'n Drive in L.A. The happy couple hit the road, all the way to Boston, Massachusetts as quick as you can say 'I do'. Julie's folks were less than happy, and for a while the lovebirds had to lay low. But when I came along, seven months later, all ten pounds twelve ounces of me, the love-nest became a little stormy and old Don took a sabbatical. About a lifetime long.

I became Julie's one reason for living, or so she told me, and I've no reason to doubt her. She got herself a place to live, sort of, in one of the termite tenements of Dorchester, Mass. She got work downtown, too, as – you guessed it – a cocktail waitress. That was in an area known as the Combat Zone, and by all accounts my mother spent much of her time there at war. Some battles she won and some she lost, which was about par for the course in that part of the world. Suffice it to say, for a good-looking seventeen year-old with a new baby, she did a damn fine job. We survived, the two of us against the rest of the known world, and before you could say 'school' I made it to five years of age almost unscathed. Those first years for me, like most kids, were a mixture of pain and pleasure. The good times were the mornings and the early evenings when the two of us would just hang. We'd go to the Common if it was fine; take a picnic and go for a trip in the swan-boats or maybe just watch the cops riding by on their giant horses. If it rained, we'd take a bus to the Science Museum and gaze up at the airplanes – I can see them now, hanging from the roof like huge dead flies in a massive spider web. But best of all was the Franklin Park Zoo.

To see the real thing, close up and in Technicolor 3-D, just blew me away. I clearly remember easing my small hand through the bars and rubbing the hard hairy horn of a giant male rhinoceros. I suppose the poor beast was more than likely blind, deaf and dumb, but to me it was like I was somewhere in Africa, out there in the dusty bush. Just me and old Horny. Then there was Magnus, the great sleepy lion, bored beyond care I guess, but not just a picture in a book. Magnus was the *real* thing. As for the monkeys, the birds and all the rest, I couldn't get enough of them, and I remember bawling my eyes out whenever it was time to go.

But especially I recall the quiet times at home with Julie. Just her and me stuffing popcorn, curled up together on the couch watching a Western and me feeling… just feeling loved, I guess. I'd gaze up at her from time to time, at her blue eyes and the blonde wavy hair that framed her pretty face like a picture. Often she'd put a blues record on the old turntable: Sonny Boy Williamson, T-Bone Walker, Albert King, Billy Holiday. Julie loved the blues and made a fair hand at singing along too. I'd hear those songs for years afterwards. Especially Albert. *If it wasn't for bad luck…* She'd tell me stories too, and speak soft, strong words to me.

'Danny-boy,' she'd say, 'we're gonna make it. What we gonna do?' I'd tell her, 'Yes mom, we're gonna make it all right, just me and you!' And then the hand of the clock would always get to the seven and she was gone. At first I used to cry and scream, but in the end I accepted the fact that I wouldn't see her until morning. And, worst of all, that I would have to spend the rest of my awake time with the Dragon.

The Dragon was a sixty year-old Irish woman, with an accent and an attitude that belonged more to the Magdalene Laundries than a Boston tenement. I've forgotten her real name now, but to me she was always a fire-breathing monster. She lived two floors below us and my mother paid her to come and sit with me and put me to bed. Sounds simple? Well it might have been, but have you ever been put to bed by a dragon? When my mother went out the door, dressed to kill for the pathetic patrons of Molly's Shamrock Bar, I was left standing behind the dirty black dress of my minder. As soon as the door clicked shut I would begin to shake. The Dragon would turn to look at me and say nothing for a moment, just shake her head and mutter, 'Tut, tut, tut.' And then she would begin, quietly at first, but always getting louder and louder until the last words were like mad screams.

‘…and you’re a dirty little boy, what are you Daniel? A filthy, Devil-loving creature! Get down on your knees now and pray! Pray for forgiveness from the Lord-your-Master. Pray to be saved from the fiery pits of Hell! Pray… boy… *PRAY!*’ And with each ‘pray’ she would smack her wrinkled old hand around the back of my head, not hard enough to break it, or even to leave a lasting mark, but hard enough to bring tears to my eyes. And then she would make me kneel on the hard timber floor until I thought I would die there. Just keel over and die from the pain in my knees and my back. It was only when she finally left me alone in my bed and I heard her clomp back to the kitchen and pour herself another tumbler of whiskey, that I could breath properly. I’d lie there for a long time, inventing elaborate curses to fill the Dragon’s remaining days on earth with pain and suffering before succumbing to the bliss of sleep.

So that’s more or less what I mean, I suppose, when I say I made it *almost* unscathed to the age of five. But when I began my sentence at Dorchester Public, I quickly understood the way things were going to be. My first beating came from Frankie Ferdinand, two years my senior and about twice my size. It was a casual affair, almost off-hand. Frankie lifted me up, spat in my face and said:

‘Hallo Irish, welcome to D.P.’ And then he battered my head against the brick wall that surrounded the school, threw me clear over it on to the pavement outside, and sauntered off. Or so I was told. All I remember is being dragged back round to the entrance and shoved through the gate with the words:

‘Ain’t no good tryin’ to run home sonny, you’re stuck in there for the next seven years or more.’

I never found out the name of the man who returned my semi-conscious little body to the school, but he was right and he was wrong. I ran home many times that first year, sometimes managing to stay free for the whole day. But I was stuck there all right. And I learnt how to survive in the maelstrom of spics, polacks and micks, most of whom were older and bigger than me for that first year, and much more experienced in the delights of torture. In time I became the same as them in a way, I suppose; no better and no worse. The only difference was that I rapidly out-grew my school buddies, and by year three there were surprisingly few left who were interested in trying to blacken my eye. Whether it was pure genetics, or whether I was some kind of freaky throw-back, by the time I was ten I’d topped six feet and was nearly as wide. The gangs all wanted me of course – naturally enough I could be of considerable use, even at that tender age. But I would have none of it, and as a consequence spent a lot of time on my own. The only gang I gathered around me, and not out of choice, were the pathetic lowest orders that exist in all communities. The too-fat, the too-small and the too-weird followed me around like I was the Pied Piper. They got to know that the one thing that made me boil was the sight of a weakling being picked on by a hulking bully, and so stuck close for protection. But if they got too near, I growled, they scattered, and I was left to my own devices once more.

And then came the day when I lost the only constant in my life. The one entity in the world that accepted me for what I was with a full and open heart. I'll never know the full story of my mother's death, and I don't want to. I only know what I was told, and that was bad enough.

That Saturday night I watched as usual as Julie Macnamara stretched her arms high and pulled on her tight black dress, tugging it down over her slim-round body until it perched about six inches above her knees. Looking at herself sideways in the mirror, she held her breath, drawing in her belly as far as she could.

'You look great Mom,' I said, 'just like … like Marilyn Monroe,' and she turned and smiled up at me.

'Sometimes I think you're the only one who thinks so, Danboy. That bastard Kelly told me I was getting fat the other night. Mind you, he's probably just thinking of a way to pay me less. If you knew what some of my *customers* call me,' she said, almost spitting the word, 'you'd go down there and tear them limb from limb, ten years old or not.' She looked me up and down. 'My God Danny, d'you suppose you're ever going to stop growing? We'll have to get a bigger house soon!'

'Dunno, Mom. You have to go tonight?'

'Ah, Danboy. You know the answer to that one. You have a good sleep honey. Tomorrow's Sunday and you and me are going out. I'm gonna get you the biggest Whippy in town. No dammit, two of them, and then we're gonna go to the zoo. What d'you say, Danbo?'

'Sure Mom, the zoo'll be great,' I told her, though both of us knew that I'd give up all the trips in the world if she could only quit work. She reached up and tousled my hair, grabbed her bag and coat and opened the door.

'See you later Danboy,' she said, and whisked out of my sight and out of my life forever.

The Dragon still used to baby-sit me at that time, but things had changed a bit by then. She never stopped roaring hellfire at me, but she no longer dared to touch me. If she tried to get me on my knees, I'd just turn my back on her, go in my room and shut the door, leaving her squawking to herself.

That night had started pretty much the same as any other. I lay in bed and waited until the Dragon's raving gave way to mumbling as the whiskey kicked in, then got swallowed up altogether by the TV. Turning over, I said my usual prayer: 'God please kill the Dragon and Kelly and let Mom stay home,' and knew no more.

Jerked awake by a hammering on the front door closely followed by a cackling scream from the Dragon, I leapt out of bed, opened the door a crack, and peeped through. Two cops were standing in the doorway, and as one of them spoke softly and hesitantly to the Dragon, she glanced over to my room. It was the only time I was to see any trace any compassion on that old witch's face, and it was a lot scarier than any of her screechings and beatings.

The cops informed me, in a gently clumsy way, that I was now an orphan. In a couple of sentences they let me know that the only reason for my existence on earth was no longer around. Just like that. Years later I was to get a little closer to the truth about what happened that Saturday night. It went something like this.

Julie had arrived at the bar on time as usual. She had donned the sexy little bonnet, mandatory wear for the waitresses in Molly's, and gone straight to work. It was early and the bar was sparsely decorated with its normal quota of drunks and wasters. Molly's at that time was like a badly lit cave, a smidgeon of hazy daylight creeping reluctantly in whenever someone opened the door. Apart from a single neon strip behind the counter, the only light was a dull electric glow coming from the plastic leprechauns that crouched in the corners of the room like evil trolls. They were barely bright enough to illuminate the faces of the nearest of the clientele, which was no bad thing. An ancient and hopeless 'Free Ireland' banner hung above the bar counter, dirty, tattered and faded. Amongst the bottles on the shelf below was a cracked glass frame with the just-readable legend: 'May You Be in Heaven Before the Devil Knows You're Dead.' Even the smell was predictable: stale beer, tobacco smoke, sweat and urine.

Slapping away a feeble attempt by one of the bums to feel her up as she cleared the rickety tables of their empties, Julie didn't notice the arrival of a different sort of customer. If she'd looked around at that stage, she would have seen a thin, nervous, pale-faced man, dressed in a cheap black suit and hat, walk in and scan the place with quick, darting glances. Apparently satisfied, he held the door open for a second man, whose entry was in total contrast to the hesitancy of the other. Shorter, stouter and more expensively clothed, he waded purposefully through the tables until he found an empty one on the side facing the doorway. Drawing an immaculate white handkerchief from a top pocket, he spread it out on the cracked leatherette and sat down, scowling at Skinny until he quickly settled himself nearby. Julie had noticed the newcomers by then and, forcing her face into a welcoming smile, walked over.

'Welcome to Molly's Shamrock Bar,' she said. 'What may I get you gentlemen?'

The fat man stared at her.

'What I want,' he said, his toneless voice unexpectedly high, 'is you.'

1st Chapter of a Creative Non-fiction Book: 2nd Prize
Cameron Dexter

Death Divides Two Towns

On May 11, 2007, a rebellious young man, a hard-charging police officer and a paranoid ex-military recluse collided on a sleepy New Hampshire road in an explosion of anger, hatred and lethal force. The repercussions of this encounter, in the shadow of a weathered white barn, echo to this day as many residents still wonder if the tragedy was avoidable or inevitable. The following is the true story of this clash between Liko Kenney, Cpl. Bruce McKay and Gregory Floyd, Sr.

May 11, 2007

The sunroof is open and the rhythms of reggae blend with the rush of highway wind as Liko Kenney and Caleb Macaulay head home after a day of work. It's 5:30 pm on a mild, mid-May New Hampshire afternoon. The two young men wear matching green Merrill's Agway T-shirts and dirty Carhart work pants. Smoke floats from their mouths and dissipates quickly with every drag of their hand-rolled American Spirit cigarettes.

Liko drives, his loosely tied, flaming red hair falls behind his back. Strands swirl around his face; a few try to escape out the driver's window. Caleb looks over at his friend. Even in the shadows, Liko's puffy cheeks and the pocks on his skin stand out. Though just 24, Liko is already a wide-shouldered, hard-living mountain man; a rage-against-the-machine man with bright brown eyes that hint of a fearsome, untameable spirit.

Caleb runs fingers through his own short, dark-brown hair. He feels sticky and dirty and looks forward to a shower. Three years younger than Liko, Caleb still has an innocence about him. Perhaps it's the layer of baby fat not quite shed. Perhaps it's that he's just an ordinary 21-year old from an un-extraordinary background.

For several months now, the two young men have toiled away at Agway in the town of Littleton, New Hampshire. For those unfamiliar with Littleton (virtually everyone), it's a random collection of 'Big Box' stores, car dealers, a movie theatre, chain restaurants, antique shops and residences strung out along the Ammonoosuc River and Rte 302 in the northern reaches of the Granite State. It's also the only place for miles to find a job.

The two sit back and relax, satisfied that a day of providing customers with gardening tools, lawn care tips and flower recommendations is over. They plan for a well-deserved night of grilling, drinking, loud music and maybe a spin on Liko's ATV.

On their way out of town, Liko and Caleb stop at the State Liquor Store and pick up a cheap bottle of vodka then toss it in the back seat. Set for the night. The drive south to Liko's home in Easton takes around 20 minutes. The only traffic they'll likely face on the trip down I-93 is a wayward moose and perhaps a police cruiser idling among roadside trees. They take neither lightly.

Two-plus hours north of Boston, Easton, NH shares borders with the towns of Sugar Hill and Franconia in the White Mountains. Of the three, Franconia is the best known, primarily as the former location of the state's legendary symbol, the Old Man of the Mountains. Sadly, the Old Man came crashing down during a storm in the spring of 2003 but its craggy, unmistakable visage remains prominent state-wide.

Easton, on the other hand, sits under the radar. Were it not for the town's famous free-spirit/athlete, US and Olympic ski racer Bode Miller, few outside the area would know the place exists. Seven miles south of Franconia, Easton is relatively flat with a couple of working farms, scattered, well-kept homes, plus a one-engine fire department and town hall. Compared to residents of Sugar Hill and Franconia, the 1,000 or so people who call Easton home might well be considered on the 'fringe' in every sense of the word.

'Eastoners' are generally content to live peacefully amid the dense woodlands, small gardens and tree-rimmed pastures. It's a place where you're as likely to ask the neighbour for a cup of milk as drive the seven miles to town for a gallon. In Easton, dogs roam off leashes, moose wander into yards, and wood fires, together with patchwork quilts, are a common cure for cold fronts. It's quiet, minimalist and private… and that's just the way the townsfolk like it, including Liko Kenney.

Yet, Liko was unique… even for Easton. He took the desire for privacy to the very edge, many would say to the point of paranoia. Somehow, Liko's world had grown from a place where boyhood wonder took him up mountains, along forest trails and finally down to some dark place only he could inhabit. After 24 years, he'd acquired the items deemed necessary to support his hermit lifestyle including a blow gun with metal darts, a chainsaw, an ATV and his latest purchase, a large-calibre hand gun.

Heading south on I-93, Liko tries to stretch his sore back while Caleb picks at the dirt beneath his fingernails. The scenic land slides by unnoticed. They've spent their lives among these clapboard villages, granite mountains, and endless stands of green. So much so that scenery which might otherwise leave a first-time visitor wide-eyed is nothing new. In fact, it's getting old.

Still, their lives are coming together. After years cruising through upstate New Hampshire and life, while friends and families wondered what they'd do with their time on earth, it seemed they finally had a plan. It wasn't anything amazing but it was something, and it was all their own. Before next winter, they'd pack their belongings (not much between them really) and head west to Oregon. They'd live off the land; raise chickens and hell, drink beer and ski every day. The young men couldn't wait.

'Let's pick up some mixers and hamburger at Mac's,' Caleb suggests, sucking on a freshly-rolled butt and pulling Liko back to the present.

'Yeah, man,' Liko says. 'Fire up the grill, and a couple fatties…'

Caleb nods in agreement as Liko swings off the highway and aims his beat, blue Celica toward Mac's: Franconia's entirely adequate, conveniently located market.

At roughly 5:45 pm, they park out front. A 4X4 Chevy Silverado pulls into the space next to them. Inside the colossal vehicle sit Gregory Floyd and his son Gregory Floyd Jr. They've stopped to pick up relish for the fish Mrs Floyd has planned for dinner. Floyd Jr. notices the two men docked alongside, then watches them walk into the store. Young Gregory is certain he recognizes them, but his mind quickly jumps to the magazines and candy daddy will buy for him today.

Though now eighteen, Greg Junior's days hardly revolve around the events, sports, girls and life normally associated with high school. Instead, he's home schooled, keeps mostly to himself and spends time with his family at their large log cabin buried in the Easton woods.

Despite the Floyds' rural location, the family is a constant source of gossip for neighbouring townsfolk. Topics include the fact that neither Mr nor Mrs Floyd seems to work (they live off disability checks) and Floyd senior's occasional appearances in local newspapers for crimes ranging from drug conviction to assault to threatening citizens with all manner of less than cordial behaviour.

Early on, the parents yanked Floyd Jr. out of elementary school after his teacher recommended he receive extra help outside the classroom. An outraged Floyd senior stormed the school and demanded to see the principal, Gail Hannigan. When her secretary, Joyce Evans, tried to stop him, Floyd threatened to put Joyce in a body bag and barged into Hannigan's office. Floyd Junior's formal education was over and Principal Hannigan, convinced her safety was now at risk, had an emergency exit built into one corner of her office.

Minus school, young Floyd grew up listening to his father's long-winded war stories in which the man invariably played hero. He spoke in whispers and often said, 'I've killed many men,' evidently because, 'the world is a dangerous place… and that's why there are guns in the house.' No matter the police said there weren't supposed to be guns in the house. But that's another story.

Near 6 pm, while the four men shop at Mac's, Cpl. Norman Bruce McKay III is driving south on Rte 116 towards Easton and Liko's home. Known less than fondly in the surrounding towns as 'McKay', he is the third member of the Franconia Police Department. Just a couple more hours and his shift/day will be over.

For McKay, May, 11 2007 began, as did every day, with getting his nine year old daughter, Courtney, off to school. He makes sure her lunch is packed and her homework stowed in the appropriate folder. He watches her climb on the bus then settles down to coffee and the local weekly newspaper, The Littleton Courier.

For the last three years, the officer lived in the nearby town of Landaff with his red-headed fiancée, Sharon Davis. They share a modest yellow home with the six white German Shepherds the two had raised with a little too much pride. They plan to marry in August (the couple, not the dogs) and talk briefly about the day ahead… how late will Bruce be working… will he be home for dinner? Sensing her boyfriend's mind is clouded by other thoughts, she leaves him to his paper. She knows McKay recently posted a memo at the station cautioning the other officers about Liko Kenney. Less than a month later, some will be wondering if McKay forgot his own warning. The following is an excerpt from that notice.

'Kenney is known to own a .45 calibre semi-automatic handgun. Kenney has both a drug history and a history of resisting arrest or detention. This notice is for informational purposes only in the event an officer is working an incident involving Kenney. 4/25/07 Cpl. Bruce McKay Reporting.'

Officer McKay's typical workday starts around noon. He makes the 'rounds' then heads to the elementary school near the centre of Franconia. Every day, a cruiser parks in the same place so an officer can keep an eye out for the children leaving school and the traffic rolling through town. It isn't the most exciting part of the job, but that's life for a small-town cop. Not a lot of action for sure. And Bruce McKay craved action.

During his ten years with the Franconia PD, McKay had 13 official complaints filed against him… no small accomplishment in such mellow surroundings. People often reported that McKay was hostile, arrogant and overly aggressive. (One woman went so far as to recommend McKay receive a complete psychological evaluation.) In spite of nauseating numerous locals, he received nearly 30 commendations during his time on the force.

McKay makes sure all the children are safely on their way then continues his afternoon rounds. Between getting ready for his upcoming marriage and the information that Liko now has a gun, he has a lot on his mind. After an hour or so, he heads back to the station and bangs out some paperwork. At 5:30 pm, he rolls off to finish his normally uneventful evening routine.

He cruises out the Easton Valley Road (Rte 116) and pulls over on Wells Road, a side street about two miles south of Franconia just before a dangerous 90-degree right turn. He switches his radar on, and waits for speeding vehicles; a frequent problem along this stretch of road.

A couple of minutes later, a car passes him heading towards Easton. McKay clocks the vehicle doing 54 mph in a 40 zone. Despite its speed, he easily identifies the car and the two men inside. Fair or unfair, small towns lead to high profiles. Franconia is no different. On this late afternoon, the vehicle tearing past, and particularly the man driving, had frequently been on McKay's figurative and literal radar screen.

Over the years, the two had clashed a number of times and it was widely known that McKay and Kenney could not stand each other. McKay clicks on the flashing blues, sirens and 'cruiser cam'. In contrast to the quiet rural road, rubber squeals and sirens scream as he takes off after Liko Kenney and Caleb McCauley.

Liko hears the all too familiar wail behind him and watches the flashing lights grow larger in his rear view mirror. Instantly, a well-known tension seizes his bones. McKay. As he searches the road for a good place to pull over, he tries to remain calm. The cop car get closer, Liko knows this is trouble.

'You should just pull over dude,' Caleb offers nervously. He understands too well Liko and McKay have a terrible past and doesn't want this latest confrontation to spin out of control. A mile on, Liko finds a decent place to stop. The two wait anxiously for the blue lights to pull in behind them. Liko can't calm down. His anger swells. In fact, he's near panic. Caleb can see Liko's hands turning white from strangling the wheel.

McKay steps out of his car, slams the door and walks to the driver's side of Liko's car. He presses close to the open window. 'Licence and registration,' he says as only a cop can. Liko doesn't say a word. Instead, he slowly rolls up the window until just a crack remains. Only then does he speak.

'I want another officer,' he says through the slim opening.

Far as Liko knew, he had the right to request a different member of the Franconia department. He believed that McKay understood it as well. This unique arrangement stemmed from their less than gracious encounters beginning five years earlier on a snowy night in an empty parking lot. Their initial meeting left Liko cuffed on frozen pavement and McKay with a sore crotch and seriously wounded ego.

Maybe it was bad luck, maybe it was fate, but on January, 26, 2003, McKay happened by the parking lot known as Fox Hill and noticed a car with grey smoke drifting up from its stern into the dark. Fox Hill had recently been reported as a 'suspicious area' where local kids were suspected of drinking alcohol and smoking weed. Liko was doing both.

McKay turned his cruiser into the lot. Surprised by the cop car, Liko quickly put out his joint and rolled down the windows. When McKay asked to see his licence, Liko refused (bad idea) and questioned McKay's reasons for requesting it. After a drawn-out dual of words, McKay requested back-up. When officers arrived, Liko was grateful and thanked them for coming. Unfortunately, they'd been informed the suspect was being combative and, without a word, approached Liko, took him to the ground, cuffed him and bound his feet. On the way down, Liko booted McKay in the groin (bad idea #2). Liko complained of a bruised jaw, eventually declaring it had been broken, though no hospital records were found to back up his claim. From then on, the two battled constantly and a hatred of the acutest type grew in each man's heart.

As Liko sits in his car on the Easton Valley Road, with McKay's face inches away yet again, he stares at the man he believes personally responsible for all the hell in his life. Through the window, a silent battle begins. It's clear they're sizing each other up and neither man would ever back down.

Caleb glances over at his friend but doesn't dare speak. Liko persists, asking McKay for another officer. McKay informs him it's not for Liko to decide. Desperate to reach a witness who could come down to the scene in case things go wrong, Liko pokes at the numbers on his cell phone. But, as with many rural areas, coverage is sketchy at best. He fails to get through.

McKay doesn't say anything and walks back to his cruiser. At 6:05 pm he radios dispatch and asks for backup. He gets confirmation that the Sugar Hill unit, Officer Phil Blanchard, is on his way.

Before McKay has time to get out and tell his quarry another officer is coming, Liko stomps on the gas and takes off down the road; desperately, wildly speeding along the familiar lane of his childhood. Had Liko waited a moment longer he would have learned that McKay had granted his request. But right now, all the desperate young man can think of is reaching the Franconia/Easton border where McKay's jurisdiction ends and Liko's imagined freedom on family land awaits.

Instinctively, McKay floors his cruiser and radios dispatch that he is now in pursuit of the blue Celica heading southbound towards Easton on 116. Beginning at 6:09 pm dispatch repeatedly calls McKay to inquire about the chase. Dispatch receives no response.

Minutes later Liko Kenney, Caleb Macaulay, Cpl. Bruce McKay and Gregory Floyd would be involved in a collision of vehicles and gunfire from which only two would walk away. The quiet NH towns of Franconia and Easton would quake along old fault lines of speculation and mistrust. And the blood stains settling into the dirt and pavement beside a sagging white barn would discolour relationships between families, factions and government officials for years to come.

Poetry: 2nd Prize
Susan Nyikos

Inscription Found in Rilke

… she comprehended nothing and said softly: 'Who?'
Rilke, Orpheus. Eurydice. Hermes. Trans. A.S. Kline

I buy the book online described as 'note inside,
handwritten, otherwise like new'
two dollars and seventy-two cents plus shipping,
no sign of wear from shelf or hands or eyes –
slightly fermented binding glue and dust trapped
between sixty-one pages, weighs a little more
than a pheasant's egg, travels with me
to the southern Utah mountains over
spring break. From the porch, where I open
the book, a two hundred seventy degree view
of raging red lust petrified in time against cerulean
sky. In blue ink on the back of the cover page:
Kay, this is perhaps my favorite poet.
I hope you enjoy it also. Mike. Feb 14, 98

This is *the strange mine of souls:* Kay and I
and Mike. Shall we forever wander, gently
rocking, one far behind the other touching
and not-touching from across time?

What if she never read your words in blue ink?
But if she did – you lucky bastard –
did she mold your picture from gray rocks
and rose petals? Did she breathe you in from fresh
glue that binds? Did she dream herself rooted yet
wandering between a quickening god and your cunning
lyre? Did her rosebud ever blossom for you? What if
she read the poems, but forgot them, all, letter by black letter?

Did her love weigh more than a pheasant's egg?

Oh Rainer Maria, no more red in the netherworld,
no new fate for Love, for Eurydice, no bodies
folded into one another like a full-bosomed tea
rose, just a moment of still *relief* chiselled
into gray marble veins, that one moment before
dark passages close and enclose her, the beloved,
newly virginal, her root fingers firmly enshrouded
in fertile rocky soil, her blossom never to open
to any lyre's song.

Did you turn around, Mike?

1st Chapter of a Creative Non-Fiction Book: Runner-up
Amanda Montei

The House with the Red Door

My mother writes to me now because I've asked her to. This is actually true. I want to know everything about everything and there are things she can't always talk about so she writes me letters, puts them in the mail, and I think she does this the old-fashioned way because it feels more glamorous to her. Or maybe more intimate. There is something attractive to her about helping me create this story, because the story has always been everything to her, and I think this is why I now feel it must be everything to me.

I read these papers and I want to find the perfect way to write back to her.

Should I start with the first memory? I had a dream once that everyone I knew was telling me their first memories. And I was saying, no you're wrong, because there were memories you made before that but you weren't old enough at the time for them to stick.

I am pushing a vacuum, I think. My parents started me on the vacuum early. I am waddle-young. Fat-face little towhead. I'm pushing my plastic vacuum but I'm probably not understanding why I have been given a vacuum to play with, since the housekeeper does all the work around the house. I am imagining that I am the housekeeper. Next to this one, the clear picture of holding a bobby pin to a door lock, pretending to use it as a key. Thinking of myself as a working woman coming home from a long day. These realities were years apart, but now they sit next to each other in the small space childhood occupies in my mind. Also, there is cooking in my play kitchen. It has a microwave, a stove that looks like its metal coils are always burning hot, a little plastic refrigerator. Inside there is plastic fruit, a plastic steak and a plastic bottle of milk. I'm salivating over it all.

Then, I'm standing in the foyer of our Hollywood Hills house. I'm crying and I'm still small. I have thrown my dress up in the air and it is caught now on the chandelier. Why did I throw my dress up in the air? I don't know. In exultation. In anger. For attention. Why does a little girl do anything? But now the dress is burning, hard up against the light bulb. A special bulb that looks like a candle flame. My older sister is there, comforting me. The housekeeper, Teresa, is there too. She is going at the dress with a broom, standing at the top of the stairs so she can reach the chandelier, and I'm below, in the foyer, my hands open like I'm telling someone I love you this much and I'm waiting for my burning dress to return to me.

My mother says her first memory is of her grandfather leaving her while she was going to the bathroom. Her grandfather died before she was born, so she never knew him. But he was always with her, she says, until one day, when she was sitting on the toilet, he came to her, told her that she was getting too old for him to be hanging around like this and that he had to leave her for good now.

I interrogate my mother about such things but it gets me nowhere. 'What do you mean he came to you?' I say. 'Like a ghost?'

'He came to me.'

'He talked to you?'

'He talked to me.'

So this story begins with ghosts. With this little girl on the toilet, a little girl named Elizabeth. And her twin sister Melissa. When they are older, they will not be able to pick themselves out in childhood pictures because they are always dressed in matching outfits. As girls, they spend their afternoons riding around the immaculate streets of Hancock Park in their red surrey, the one with the fringe. The lawns slope up around them, spilling onto stately porches, front doors bigger than need be. They come home and watch their older sister draw circles in the air with her pointed toes above the backyard diving board, above the Olympic-sized pool. Her swimming cap has a fringe, too. Their older brother makes regular appearances on *Father Knows Best* and their father is a big time Hollywood producer, and when their parents invite photographers into the home for family pictures, they pose with Benny, the black man in the white suit who drives their father to Paramount studios every morning, and Macy, the black woman who cooks all the family meals. On the weekends, their parents host soirees and whisky-ice-clinking evenings with Conrad Hilton, Ricky Nelson and the man who would eventually cancel *The Smothers Brothers*.

I interrogate my mother about this too because memory has a fragility that begs interrogation. And because I see my mother's mind as a fuzzy clouded thing. Warped by years of wanting to go back to those days, that big house, that red surrey.

I think of all the coffee table books my mother had of Monet's watery scenes, because coffee table books are important to have out for company. *Water Lilies*. Yes, I think what she sees of her past now is liquid and blurry just like that.

She tells me one day, 'We had Reagan over you know.'

'Reagan? Really.'

'I think we had Reagan over in those days. All the time, I think.'

'*Really*?'

'Yes, I think so.'

These fancy people moved about the living room weightless, starlets with furs and red lips drooping down long wet loose faces, bodies hanging on the arms of chairs. The twins were called on to perform songs and skits, mix drinks, and then just get out of the way.

Before my parents divorced, my mother and father worked in a studio managing and producing records for fledgling artists and they made enough to put us up in the huge house in the Hollywood Hills. In my mind, I am perpetually in a white and gold dress with a lace collar. My sister is in her favourite dress too. A red velvet one, also with a lace collar. We were matching, lace-collared people then.

'Remember on Viewmont the way I used to brush your hair and you would cry and cry?' My mother speaks of life as though it were nothing without nice street names. She has come to understand her life as a series of houses, each with their own mood, their own sense of rebirth and subsequent abandonment. The Viewmont days were the best, because we had everything. A two-storey house tucked in the Hollywood Hills that overlooked Los Angeles, my room with a view of the entire skyline. My parents' room then was something frightening, something I was too young to experience. My parents, in a way, were like that too. They always left the house in fur and leather, and I always asked them to bring me something home, to please just stay with me one night.

But they did leave and I spent my free time with Teresa and I became very good at ordering her around. '*Queso en plato, por favor*,' I would say, and snap my fingers the way I had seen rich white people do on TV. And she would shred cheddar cheese onto my favourite Little Mermaid plate and put it in the microwave and I would suck on the greasy results while watching my parents' Laser Discs.

But okay there were some good times with your father I GUESS. If I have to admit it. He was an amazing guitar player. When I was a teenager you know I ran away from home and I stayed with your father in his little Honda car. We just slept in the back and parked in grocery store lots. I stayed with him at his mother's house for a while but when she found out that my parents were upset she would not have any of that. She was one tough woman I'll give her that. But of course I loved him or thought I loved him. I was young and he played the guitar so well although he never once wrote me a song. What's that all about?

After I ran away your father's band ClearRock started doing quite well. It was his band and this ehem little known band called VAN HALEN duelling at the Whisky A Go Go on Sunset every weekend. VAN HALEN! Heard of them? I thought so! And I swear your father's band was beating them out in ticket sales ALL THE TIME. They were really something and I loved being the girl with the band getting high all the time. Oh man it was really fun just to feel so young and free. But then your father up and decided he wanted to move to Hawaii just like that and of course we did although I knew it was a terrible idea. His drummer, well I'm not sure if it's a story you're interested in because it's kind of sad, but his drummer started drinking heavily when we moved to Hawaii. It was really sad to watch Jim spiral like that and I still feel it only happened because we moved from LA to Hawaii where there is just nothing to do but drink and get high. That's just the way things ended up, it's such a relaxed place and within a year he had overdosed and I will say that in some way I still blame your father for that because I think if we had stayed in LA it never would have happened.

In the Hollywood Hills house, my parents owned a four-poster bed that we sold to the studios and was later used in the movie Maverick. It was always tit for tat, my mother says about her marriage to my father. This is years later and we are sitting at the yellow table in the house with the red door, which I'll tell you about, and we are getting high but what she says next ruins the feeling.

'If I wanted new shoes, it was, "Okay, only if you let me tie you to the bedpost."'

'You shouldn't tell me these things,' I say. 'How many times have I told you that you shouldn't tell me these things?'

'Well it's true,' she says.

'But don't you see why you probably shouldn't tell me these things?'

'What-ever.'

In the same way we once bathed together, we wade around in language and memories and try to re-frame all that we know about ourselves and each other. It is, in fact, just another kind of innocent nakedness.

I'll tell you about the nail in the coffin but I don't ever want to talk about this again. I went to your father who was standing in front of the mirror in the bathroom in the Hollywood Hills house. He was in front of that looooong mirror in the bathroom doing something I can't imagine what, styling his hair maybe, I don't know. Probably brushing his teeth. And I put my hand on his shoulder and I looked at him in the mirror and he was well over three hundred pounds at that point and definitely high as usual and I said, 'Bill.' And I must have been crying. I said, 'Bill you know I don't love you, right?' And do you know what he said? He said patting me on the shoulder like I hadn't even said anything, 'That's okay, I love you enough for the both of us.'

When my mother first left my father, she was beautiful and exciting. We rented a new condo by the studios and on the weekends we lay by the pool with her comedian friends, who told jokes and smoked cigarettes and flirted with her. I tried to get them to flirt with me. She was managing them then, and spent nights at the Laugh Factory and yes, it's so many years later that I learn why she was so skinny then and when I do learn, the reality of her is punctured like black paper, light leaking in.

One night, I watched my mother pile her hair on her head as I clomped around in the golden glitter shoes that I can never shake from my mind, and I said, 'Mom, your hair's messy.' She laughed knowingly, and assured me it was intentional. I cried when she left that night, feeling stupid and young.

Some nights, when my mother was out, I sat at her big glass desk in the dining room but I did not pretend to be her. I ignored the headshots all around me and put on her fancy telephone headset and played my favourite game, 1-800-DENTIST. I helped people with achy teeth find the best dentist in their area. In her room, I shuffle through her magazines and find *Playboys* under her bed. When I ask her about them, she will tell me that she buys them for the articles, really good articles. Years later, I'll wonder if there was mockery in her voice when she said this, and I'll feel bitter with betrayal and disgust. I won't ever tell her how many vibrators I found and experimented with and I won't ever want to think of her as a sexual creature, too afraid to see any more abnormalities in her.

In that condo, the Bic hung from the shower organizer like the Grail. These were days when I slept in my mother's bed nearly every night and my older sister made fun of me for it. These were days when I still bathed with my mother, still felt awed by the beauty of her body.

I sit in the bathtub with my mother and she explains to me why I don't really want to start shaving my legs so young, even if the other girls already are.

'Once you start you'll be doing it for the rest of your life,' she says. 'Every day. Every single day and when you don't you'll be prickly and manly.' I decide I will shave my legs when she isn't around.

I duck under the water and pretend to be a fish and she giggles. We are naked and nothing is strange about that yet. I want to be as close to her as possible. We play a game called Drop the Soap. 'Where's the soap baby?' And she grabs my foot and rubs it on her arm, her face.

'That's not the soap mommy! It's my foot!' She thinks I'm funny and I revere her. We get out of the bath and dry off as fast as possible. She says the faster you get the water off the faster you get warm. I never forget this. Sometimes, she gets hot towels from the dryer. This time, she looks in the mirror and she has left me. She has her fingers all over her face.

'I'm so tired of being ugly,' she says.

I know her polyps, the ones between her legs. Does this make you uncomfortable? That I know of bumps in such an intimate place? My grandmother told her they came from being unclean. My mother says, 'Your grandmother was always faulting me,' and my mother says this with her head wobbling like a bobblehead. Years later, her shakes will make me feel like she is an invalid to be hidden from the world, until the first time I see black-and-white Katherine Hepburn shivering away.

I never knew who to believe about the polyps.

Another game of Drop the Soap. My mother tells me she will have a cone put up in her uterus to scrape out the lining. It's some sort of test for uterine cancer, she says. She has to be picked up from the hospital by a friend, she will be in bed for a few days. I worry, but the test ends up being negative.

Another night in the bathroom she's on the toilet fondling her polyps absentmindedly. 'You know when I went to the doctor it was because I was pregnant, right sweetie?'

I say, 'You're pregnant?'

And she says, 'Not any more, sweetie.'

I do think about that little baby. I can't say I think about that little baby every day but I think there was definitely a time when I did. This was before Jonathan moved in with us and yes I know you don't remember him living in the condo but whatever. He did. Don't you remember him telling us to get off our asses and clean the house? He was such a wonderful dancer though and we had so much fun together. I felt so new then. I had never had a man love me like that. Your father and I never DANCED!

But the little baby was before that. It was, well it doesn't matter who the guy was, you met him though. It was very unexpected and very frightening and I felt so alone when I went to the doctor. I knew I couldn't tell you girls because you were so young and your sister was already feeling resentful about me leaving your father and working so much. But what choice did I have? I could hardly support the three of us and your father of course never paid child support on time if at all.

I do remember telling you in the bathroom that I had it done. I think it was silly of me and I feel awful about it now. You were too young to hear about such things. I may have just wanted to get it off my chest and I knew you wouldn't really understand at that age. You have to understand how hard it is when you have no one in the world to just say things out loud to.

Short Story: Runner-up
Miranda Landgraf

Scotch Corner

Three children and their mother are in a Hillman Imp on the southbound carriageway of the A1, travelling at a dogged sixty the slow way south.

Above the hills of Yorkshire, the morning is darkening for rain. Loose in the back, the youngest pair are waving at lorry drivers from the boot.

The eldest child is fifteen and has the back seat to himself. Dressed in brown cord trousers and a plaid shirt, Pete's gaze is fixed on the banks and scrubby planting that line the side of the road.

Marion, at the wheel, has inherited Pete. She has often wished his mother was estranged rather than dead, because the estranged continue to show their imperfections, whilst the dead do not. And Pete's loyalty, even after a decade, remains unassailable. The boy yearns for his mother still.

Driving past the signpost for Durham, Marion glances at the empty passenger seat. She and the family have been invited to spend time with her mother in the south. It was an invitation extended to all of them, and though her husband, John, has pleaded work, Marion is still thinking of excuses she may give.

Already it has been a long morning.

And there are hundreds of miles still ahead.

Watching the dash lines on the road fall behind her, Marion wonders whether she has unplugged the iron. Whether it is even off.

Pete leans over and snatches the book Jane is reading between the gaps in lorry drivers. Jane is nine, and yells for him to give it back.

Marion glances in the rear view mirror.

'Give it back!'

Pete is wearing a smile.

'Give the book back,' says Marion again.

She no longer has the rope for a slow build.

'Otherwise you'll be walking.'

What follows is the girn of children who want to progress an issue without its progression being noted by those in charge.

'Why don't we play I went to the market?' asks Marion. 'Tom, you start.'

Tom, aged six, still loses his place in the middle of the alphabet and is relieved to go first.

'I went to the market,' he shouts from the boot, 'and I bought an apple.'

Pete groans.

'I went to the market,' says Jane, 'and I bought an apple, and a bear.'

Everyone waits for Pete. He glares out the window.

'Come on Pete,' says Marion, 'you used to love this.'

'I went to the market and I bought an apple, a bear, and a cock.'

Marion looks in the rear view mirror.

'I went to the market and I bought an apple, a bear, a cockerel and a doll.'

In the back, Tom is struggling to remember the words, his mind half on the lorries. Jane coaxes him on.

The round of I went to the market comes back to Pete.

'I went to the market, and I bought an apple, a bear, a cock, a doll, an egg, a flower and a gun.'

'Shall we stop for lunch?' asks Marion.

They stutter through Newton Aycliffe, groaning up the main street, hunting a parking space, or a restaurant, or both. They are almost out the other side of town before she can park.

There is much manhandling of seats to get those in the back out, and to find cagoules and umbrellas. Drizzle has flecked the pavement till it is turning slick and dark. Newton Aycliffe's Methodist church clock already reads quarter past twelve. At this rate it won't be until well after six that they arrive, and Marion's mother has a routine from which she rarely yields. Arriving late, with Pete, and without John, will not be a good start.

Behind her, Pete is reaching round the front of Jane with his foot, trying to trip her up. Jane pushes him away, and he springs out into the road, causing a car to break and honk.

'Get off the road!' Marion grabs Pete by the scruff of his shirt. 'Get off the bloody road.'

He snaps out of her grasp and saunters away. It is this ability to display her as an incompetent mother that she dislikes in Pete most. And the week ahead will be full of such judgments. Pete is like a jigsaw piece stuffed into the wrong hole. Marion's mother finds him, and his behaviour, hard to overlook.

They reach a red phone box and Marion decides she will make a call about the iron. The door is heavy, releasing a stench of urine. Tom pushes inside.

'Can I dial the number?'

She begins to sound them out.

Tom gets up on his tiptoes, but he does not have the reach to pull the nought on the dial all the way. Marion tries not to think about the time and how it is sliding away from her. Through the greasy panes of glass she watches Pete, lounging on the garden wall of someone's house.

Jane, standing outside, tugs open the door.

'Can I dial the number too?

'No. Tom's finished.'

'But that was only three numbers,' Tom whines.

Jane, more sensitive to boiling points, hauls Tom out.

Marion redials. The receptionist at Scottish Widows answers and she presses the ten pence piece home.

'Hallo? Hallo?'

'Scottish Widows.'

'Please may I speak with John Donaldson?'

'Just putting you through.'

Marion glances out towards Pete, who has taken to picking the grout out from between the bricks.

'Can I take a message? Mr Donaldson has a day's holiday.'

'I'm sorry?'

'Mr Donaldson won't be in the office today.'

'This is his wife speaking.'

'Oh, hallo Mrs Donaldson. Perhaps his secretary's mistaken. Do you want me to try again?'

'No. Thank you.'

Marion regrets having admitted she is John's wife.

'Okay, back to the car,' she says.

Pete looks up.

'I thought we were having lunch.'

'There's not time for lunch.'

'But I'm hungry,' wails Tom.

Marion strides away, up the road. The drizzle has hardened into rain.

At the Hillman, Marion sits in the front seat and watches the blurred silhouettes of her children in the windscreen mirror dragging towards the car. Tom is in front, his wet fringe dark against his face. She draws her eyes away, back to the raindrops that swell and slide over the glass.

As the children approach, Marion leans over and unlocks the passenger side. Hauling the seat forward against the dashboard, Tom and Jane scramble into the back. Their cagoules are wet, condensation whiting out the view.

It is some minutes before Pete ambles alongside. Marion pushes the passenger seat back into position.

'In the front.'

'Why can't I sit in the front?' asks Tom.

'Because.'

'I'm hungry.'

'Shh,' whispers Jane.

Pete slides in.

'I can smell pooh,' says Tom.

'Shh,' says Jane.

'Check your shoes,' says Marion for she can smell it too. 'Pete. Go on. You as well.'

'But you're not checking yours.'

'Because it did not smell of pooh when I was in here on my own.' Marion speaks without any conviction.

'It's not me,' says Tom.

'Me neither,' says Jane.

'Pete?'

He looks at her and Marion can see his own mother slide across his face. His baleful glance is a mixture of beauty and superiority that no-one else in the family can manage.

Marion turns the key in the ignition and the windscreen wipers paddle back and forth. Back. And forth. She indicates. Then pulls out into the main street of Newton Aycliffe, heading south.

'Perhaps someone's guffed,' says Jane. Though the smell is of dog and grows stronger with each minute.

Pete taps his left foot, staring at the drops that blow horizontally against the window. Marion wonders if he has brought dog shit into the car deliberately, and this tapping of his foot is a way of spreading it around.

'I'm not asking you again, Pete. Check your shoes.'

His Dunlop green flash continue to drum the floor of the car, and over the noise of the rain on the Hillman's roof, there is the faint hiss of his whistle.

'I'm hungry,' Tom calls again from the back.

Marion ignores him and leans forward towards the windscreen. The wipers are not quick enough to sweep away the rain. It boils across the glass. Signposts for Darlington slide behind them and others for the services at Scotch Corner build. And all the time there is nothing else to think of but the smell.

'Take off your shoes Pete.'

'I tell you. It's not me. It fucking smelt like shit in here before I got in the car.'

'Do not use that language with me.'

Pete traces the rain drops and their residue over the glass with a finger.

'Pete. Do as I say.'

It is then that she sees the roundabout for Scotch Corner.

Marion pulls up beneath the shelter of the petrol station, and asks the attendant for ten gallons of petrol and an empty box. When he returns from the pay shed, there is a white Wrigleys Spearmint carton in his hand.

'Tom. Have you a felt tip?'

Marion grabs the green one Jane holds out and tears the box open against her legs. Soon she is scrawling 'EDINBURGH' in block capitals across the bare cardboard.

'Mum,' Pete asks. 'What are you doing?'

'You're getting out.'

Marion scrabbles around in her purse, and pushing the sign and a ten pound note into Pete's hands, leans over to open the passenger door.

There is silence in the back.

Pete stands slowly. At the back of the car, he lifts the boot and takes his coat and bag from it. Marion turns the key in the ignition, and the windscreen wipers paddle back and forth. Back. And forth. She indicates. Then pulls out onto the slip road, heading south.

There is still the stink of dog shit, warming where it is smeared over the accelerator peddle. And now the rain is falling over the suitcases in the back, the rear door open and bouncing as the Hillman accelerates into moving traffic.

Tom clambers over into the back to wave.

Flash Fiction: Runner-up

Lunar Hine

November

It is a sear November night. Frost frightens his bones. A lifted foot could be a broken hip. He shuffles down the dark mouth of a London plane avenue and over the bridge into the poor end of town. His head, bare of all but a few hairs, butts the wind that is terrier to his old coat. He stoops, weighed down by the awkward case he carries. His crooked stick fingers are white around the handle as if frozen for all time. Slowly he reaches shuttered shops, their stained doorways empty for now. Edging around knots of people turned out of the pub, he is invisible.

He carefully descends stone steps slippery with iced piss. Opening a heavy door with his back he blinks into the muted dazzle of a club. As he crosses the floor he is greeted many times. A slap on his back makes him stumble and laugh. A drink is fetched before his coat is off. It is quiet tonight. Like him, no-one dares drive this rink. Bourbon drained and refilled, the case is opened. He takes his place on his stool, lifts his saxophone and plays. A hush surges through the room, and out on the cold street stragglers pause, dragon breath rising, to listen.

Creative Non-fiction Essay: Runner-up
Nicole Quinn

We Killed A Nun

It was 1964, my first year at the convent. It wasn't actually a convent, but rather a boarding school where Catholic girls were 'finished', turned out into the world as 'Gentlemen's ladies', a phrase, which under contemporary scrutiny, conjures a host of meanings. The school seemed out of place out of time housed there on thirty gate-enclosed acres, replete with riding trails and armed guards, smack in the middle of southern California blue collar suburban sprawl. Tiny pastel houses had sprouted around its once rural perimeter, multiplying into a relatively unremarkable city. The world had continued outside those iron gates, while all the trappings of the late nineteenth century were doggedly preserved on the inside.

Erected in 1889 and fashioned after the early missions, the convent was made up of saffron tinged stucco, tile roofs, and soaring bell towers which could be seen above mature eucalyptus groves as you whirred past on the San Bernardino Freeway, west to somewhere east to somewhere else.

We killed Sister Cordelia sometime our first year there. She was old, old enough to die, too old to teach fourth grade mathematics. Past her prime to handle ten, often unruly, little girls, let alone two sets of twins – especially if one set happened to be brown skinned.

Ria and I weren't really twins, at least not by appearance, a fact which would plague us both well into adulthood. We weren't even twins biologically. Three crucial months separated us in age, and two separate wombs had conceived us. But we had been adopted simultaneously as infants. We shared a familial neurosis, at least in the formative years, so it's not surprising that if a nun were to be killed, we would do it together.

Sister Cordelia Marie, a devoutly literary name, reminiscent of Lear's virtuous daughter, though now pickled and past her glory. Reagan and Goneril, long vanquished, were no longer there to reflect her righteous light, so she cast about for new victims on whom to wreak her venerated ire.

We sat, ten little girls, knees locked together, plaid pleats and bobby sox, as she drilled us mercilessly with rote equations, daring us to be wrong. Ria and I usually were. We had skipped grade three, that bedrock year when sets of numbers were agonizingly committed to memory. The year mathematical confidence was reinforced. We had bypassed that foundation year in order to enter the convent, which was, for economic reasons, dropping a class a year, and always the one we would have been old enough to enter. But it became urgent, that year, for us to seek safe harbour within its walls full time. We were sent there, partly, as a means of escaping the racism inherent in the small California enclave Mama and Papa had chosen to integrate only the year before.

Claremont was a college town, boasting no less than six well regarded institutions of higher learning (Pitzer, Scripps, Pomona College, C.M.C., and Harvey Mudd, as well as the Claremont Graduate School). There was housing available for non-whites at that time, somewhere on the other side of the tracks, or in this case, the Baseline, but it wasn't where Mama and Papa chose to buy their home.

Baseline was the name of the road which divided the mountains from the valleys, divided blue collar from white, white from non-white. We moved into the house just above the baseline, the pretty white house on Glen Way, with the half circle drive and the columns of scrolled ironwork, despite the petition drawn up to keep us out. We moved there sometime in the summer of 1963, under cover of darkness, with whispered voices and flash lights casting eerie beams on the newly painted walls.

We were enrolled in a local parochial school, and fared well there, academically at least, despite the school bus that refused to stop, until Mama stood in the middle of the road daring the driver to hit her. The dog faeces hurled at our cars, the dead animals in the mailbox, the garbage cans heaved at our front windows, the cold shoulders and muffled expletives from our white neighbours we took as an element of being different. We accepted it all as part and parcel of changing entrenched attitudes and racial stereotypes, because Mama said that's what we were doing, and she had a knack for making terror fun.

For months we only walked along the edges of the rooms facing the street of that new house. I thought it was to maximize the number of footsteps, thereby increasing your chances of winning her 'footstep game'. It was only later that I realized she had invented this ruse to keep us from being easy targets for any rock throwers who showed up during that first year. We were surprisingly unafraid, unscarred by the hate of those around us. At least I was, until that Valentine's card was presented to me, amid a chorus of snickers, by a ruddy-faced thug who regularly taunted my sister and me on the school bus.

The card: 'Happy Valentine's Day Nigger' was scrawled in number 2 pencil across pink card stock liberally ornamented with red hearts and silver glitter.

Ria and I would ride in the back of the bus. Not because it was mandated, but because we loved the bounce of that extra wide seat, the view out the back window, and the girls who hung with us shunning the snide remarks and projectiles heaved by that scrub brush headed kid and his cronies. They never bothered Tian, our brother. He was older than us by three years. He was a wise-ass. He could pass. They all felt sorry for the poor little white (looking) boy living in the house full of darkies. They treated him like a spy, finding out whatever they could about our 'tails' and whatever else went on in the house of which stories were already circulating in mythic proportions.

The boys on that bus had decided that Tian wasn't really one of us, no way, he didn't look like one, he wasn't no nigger. Nigger. I had heard the word, in jest or in hypothetical debates about racial constructs between my parents and their peers. But I had never seen it written down. I wasn't sure what it said on that Valentine card, but whatever it was, it had a sort of permanence in that form, like history. I endeavoured to sound it out, trying to remember what the rule was for vowels followed by a double consonant, finally taking it to Mama for a translation. Mama, who for the rest of our time in the house on Glen Way, some fifteen years, would wield that word as a means of silencing conversations at dinner which had become too raucous.

'The niggers are eating!' she would extol in the mock tones of a faceless neighbour, or in her 'Mammy' voice, and it always had the desired effect. We would sit, quietly, shame-faced, wondering if race really did have any relation to volume and unruly behaviour – imagining those tight-lipped wasps, rolling their eyes at conversations that wafted across swimming pools permeating the sangfroid elegance of their evening meals. As if being loud was another tangible sign of our inferiority. We were suckled on the stereotypes we were charged to dispel.

Mama cuddled me onto her lap that afternoon, that Saint Valentine's day when I was seven, the day I became a nigger. And perhaps that's why I recall the event at all. It was a rare luxury, a cuddle from a woman who rarely took time away from earning money. Mama had determined that our childhoods would be different from hers, that we would never want, that we would view the world from an equal footing, and she worked diligently to afford it. She'd seen her mother take extra money jobs, demeaning jobs, even as bathroom attendant at a Klan rally, and swore never to humble herself among the enemy. She worked, Special Education schools during the day, nurse at night. Sometimes 16 hours a day, double time on holidays. All to bolster the comfortable income Papa already provided as an aerospace engineer in a culture where most people of colour were still on the assembly line.

Mama had scant time for hugs. 'C.Y.K.!' was the way she normally exited the house, the initials representing the words 'Consider yourself kissed'. So the cuddle meant something, something important. And that something became the convent.

When the engraved note cards arrived, the ones inviting us to become Convent Girls, we were encouraged to be jubilant. And we were, though no one seemed to consider that we would be integrating the convent as well, nor that multiplication tables were a requisite part of grade four. Consequently, Ria and I spent all of Sister Cordelia's math class dreading the questions to which we would have difficulty providing an accurate answer.

Sister Cordelia, pruned and pinched, wimpled in stiffly starched grosgrain, would hover, just in front of each chair, firing questions on fetid breath. She was stone deaf, forcing her to focus on your mouth, her features scrunched in an angry frown, as if her whole face were required to read the answer from your lips. A correct response to any equation always seeming to disappoint her, not allowing for the justified pain she was entitled to inflict when learning was not in evidence.

The thump: a flick of the middle finger off the thumb making contact with the head at very close range, administered with a sneer of disdain. A lash: was to be flogged with the large wooden rosary, draped from her waist, held in reserve for such offences as talking out of turn, passing notes, and taking the Lord's name in vain. These were her weapons of choice. Every nun had her own personal method. Rulers, the hand, the ping-pong paddle.

Ria and I always got thumped. It seemed as if somehow, our dark skin made it harder for the teachers to teach us the harshly elegant lessons of civilized life. We were the only ones after all,

Negroes, in the whole school of three hundred girls. Two more would arrive the following year, but in the beginning it was just the Jacksons, Maria and Nico, as we were then known, the only Americans of colour in that California convent boarding school in 1964.

We certainly were not the only 'exotics' housed behind the iron gates. The armed guards were there to protect the daughters of parents whose grandeur was commensurate with their bank accounts. South American ranch owners, Panamanians, still flush with funds from the canal, Mexican cattle barons, Chinese, rife with assets from Hong Kong's healthy economy, and South Koreans who arrived with at least one suitcase filled, specifically, with spending cash.

But Ria and I spoke unaccented American English. Ria and I were the unnerving heralds of a new day. American Negroes, the descendants of slaves, who could afford the education and lifestyle heretofore proffered only to the elite and white or brown-but-foreign.

But we didn't know that's who we were. We were eight years old, little girls embarking on a new adventure, boarding school, just like the books we'd heard of English bairns shipped off to learn the ways of the world. And those ways included racism, classism, and sexism, but not yet, not among little girls. In the beginning we were all tarnished in some way. All of us were too something to be perfect ladies. Too fat, too tall, too shy, too much for our families to bear.

We didn't know that the offences of which we were accused were not of our own making. We didn't know that they were society's sins. Neither did our peers. From our point of view we were all the same. Little girls housed away from mothers and fathers, wondering if being there was gift or punishment, as both feelings held equal sway. It was the adults who had the hardest time containing the perceived differences they too had been taught. It was the nuns who waged a holy war. Religious women confronted with their own hate, their own habits, needing to rationalize them by demonizing us. It was the parents, afraid of the stigma attached to long term association. But even that we didn't comprehend. Not yet. Not then.

We killed Sister Cordelia sometime that first school year. She didn't die right away, but lingered in some malignant stupor, some threat of return, until the bells finally tolled her demise. No one blamed us. But when I look back, there seems to be no other explanation for what happened that day.

The Gilrain twins were identical in looks, though not in personality. And maybe that's what drew us together – each of us knowing what it was like to be compared to someone else, mistaken for someone else, just when you're trying to figure out who you are. It was not unusual for Patty and my sister to band together in heated feuds against Margaret and me. There were whispered taunts and name calling behind Sister Cordelia's deaf back, and when the pressure was on I could hurl an eraser across a room with speed and accuracy. And so it happened that day, as it had many times before.

Patty and Margaret, white and upper middle class, like most of the American girls we lived with nine months of the year, were products of broken homes. Boarding school, at least in our sphere, was a socially acceptable solution to custodial absenteeism, single parents, stepmothers, and as the years wore on, a moneyed alternative to reform school. Ria and I were members of an elite group at our convent, the two parent household. It afforded us a useful weapon to ward off the taint of adoption and race.

When we killed Sister Cordelia the Gilrain/Jackson factions were holding a full scale war behind the deaf woman's back. We never expected her to turn around, never when she was writing mathematical terms on the blackboard in that painstakingly parochial script, the legacy of a Catholic education. We could always count on at least a few minutes of unsupervised frenzy while she wrote the next set of torturous equations. But she did turn that day, her veil whipping out behind her, a black sail the malevolent crusader's banner.

It must have seemed a dumb show, four girls in brown and white units, button-down shirts, dishevelled desks as barricades, wads of lined paper and gummed erasers lobbed with malicious intent across giggling heads into enemy territory. Chaos reigned and we were its servants.

Sister Cordelia's face shrivelled in horror. She sputtered names, but her powers of speech failed to serve her. She pointed her bony digit, waving it across the room at us, an inquisition-style indictment of our guilt. She gasped and her eyes widened. She stared at me. I remember the pale blue of her eyes, Delft china, stippled with small red veins. She clutched at her habit, as if it were a skin that had suddenly grown too tight. The colour drained from her face, leaving it pale and wrinkled, blank parchment on which naught was writ. She wheezed a final denouncement, 'You're... killing me!' Then she crumpled a heap of black cloth, onto the wide oak desk before us.

The clock ticked. Ten pairs of owl eyes, wide and staring, mouths agape – tick, tick, a loud pulsating rhythm, rivalled only by the rabbit thumping of our hearts. We sat down. This admonishment had been unusual and extremely effective. We waited to see what the reprise to such a display could possibly be. But she didn't move, and neither did we.

Ria remembered that some of the girls ultimately fled screaming. But the four of us were loath to leave Sister Cordelia Marie alone in that room. She'd never been warm, her temperature just high enough to keep her other foot out of the grave, until that moment when we watched it drop. But in that moment we cared. There had been something naked about her actions, something vulnerable and true. We knew she shouldn't be alone.

We never talked about it after that day. We never had to explain what had happened in that classroom prior to her attack. No one asked, and we never volunteered. No one counselled us, as might have happened today in the light of any traumatic incident which is school related. Life just went on – same school, new math teacher, less thumping. We'd killed a nun, and we'd remained innocent.

1st Chapter of a Novel: Runner-up
Laura Solomon

The Theory of Networks

It's the first day of rehearsals and I'm so nervous my hands are shaking. No Green Frog to depend on now; it's all up to me. Green Frog, or GF, as he was more informally called, used to be my stuffed toy sidekick, but I burnt him last year; I outgrew him. It's early, five-thirty a.m., and nobody else in the house is awake yet. I have to be in Central, at the set, by seven, hence my pre-dawn rise. *Dark Before Dawn* is my first film. I'm excited and terrified at the same time; my nerves are on edge. When the neighbour's cat jumps up onto the windowsill, hitting its head against the pane, I nearly jump out of my skin. I sit at the kitchen table, drinking my coffee and eating my *Hubbard's Berry Berry Nice* muesli.

I will need to be on top form today, to be the best Olivia Best I can be. Who knows what this film will lead onto, if I do a good job. I'm not the kind of girl who does things half-heartedly, whatever I do, I always give it my best shot and this film will be no exception. I was talent-spotted by the director, Howard Richardson, during last year's school production, *The Tempest*, and asked to audition for the role of Charlotte. It's a meaty role, the film isn't fluffy; Howard's a big Mike Leigh fan and Leigh's influence really shows in the film. Gritty realism. *Dark Before Dawn* is about Charlotte finding out that her father is not her real father at all. Her real father is sterile, so her father's best friend, who is, by the time he contacts Charlotte, a high-flying corporate mogul in the music industry, slept with her mother, producing Charlotte. The film is about Charlotte's efforts to establish a relationship with her real father who, shortly after Charlotte's fifteenth birthday, gets in touch with Charlotte's mother to ask if he can have contact with his daughter.

I have been diligent. I have memorised all my lines, even though it was tough to get them all down pat, as I was also studying for exams at the same time. Howard timed shooting so that it starts during school holidays, but we're going to continue into the school term for another three months. It's going to be exhausting; three days a week I have to leave school half an hour early in order to be at rehearsals in time. I will have to work through till nine pm. Dinner will be provided. It's a lot for me to tackle, but I reckon I'm up to it.

I finish my breakfast, take a quick shower and change into jeans and a T-shirt. Howard told us to dress casually. Then I'm out the door and into the black cab which is waiting for me. I feel like quite the movie star, not having to take the bus. Transport is paid for. The driver tries to make small talk, but I'm not in the mood; my mind is full of my lines, and also my future possibilities. Maybe I won't be a computer geek forever, maybe I will become Olivia Best, actress. In no time at all we have arrived at the space where rehearsals are being held. It's a hall in Central London, but we're not allowed to say where because of security issues. I thank my driver, then step out and stomp up the stairs and in through the front door.

The other actors are already gathered, sitting on hard wooden chairs in a small group, chatting amongst themselves. Howard's out in front, up near the stage, riffling through some notes. I take a seat with the others and introduce myself. I've met them all before at a read-through Howard held last week. They seem like a good bunch, though most of them have a lot more experience than me and are trained actors. I'm the new girl, the unknown. It seems so unlikely that I should wind up here. I never wanted to be an actor; I'm an Ubernerd, a geek, I have an ongoing love affair with my PC. My mobile beeps. It's a text from my boyfriend Bev.

Very good luck for your first day. Call round to mine after rehearsals. X B.

I switch off my phone. It's bad manners to be beeping or texting during working hours.

Howard clears his throat.

'Okay, so we're all here. I think we can make a start. Firstly, let me all say, welcome to the first rehearsal of *Dark Before Dawn*. I'd like to introduce the producer, Kirsten James.'

'Hello,' people mutter. 'Hello Kirsten.'

'And I wanted to thank you all for being part of the film. We're going to start with another read-through and then, as per your schedule, most of you can go home, but I'd like Olivia and Jonathan to stay because we're going to be working together all day.'

Jonathan Partridge is the actor who is going to play my father, David. He's in his forties and has been around forever; he's quite well known on the London acting scene. He's been on *The Bill* and *Coronation Street* and has appeared in a number of West End productions. His experience intimidates me a bit, but I am attempting to take today in stride. There's nothing else I can do.

The read-through goes smoothly. I only fluff one of my lines and make a quick recovery. Jonathan doesn't mess anything up and hardly seems to need to look at his script. I am still a bit reliant on mine; I know my lines, but I am not quite *au fait* with how they fit in with the lines of others. I am hyper-alert, hyper-vigilant and sometimes cut in a bit too quickly, before the other person has quite finished speaking. I can feel the coffee pulsing through my system, keeping my nerves and brain buzzing. When we're done, everybody except me, Jonathan and Howard head off.

'Right,' says Howard. 'We're going to have a quick tea break – the tearooms are over to the left there, and then I think we'll get into some character development with the two of you.'

Jonathan and I make a dive for the tearooms. There's an open packet of gingernuts. I eat three in quick succession then make myself a strong cuppa, using two tea bags. I need the caffeine. Jonathan seems like a good sort; he's very down to earth and not at all up himself or luvvie. This is the first chance Jonathan and I have had to talk. Nobody hung around after the first read-through. He can sense that I'm nervous and tries to make me feel at ease by joking around, telling me about how his wife is always nagging him to settle down and get an office job.

'She'd like me in a suit and tie. But I tried that in my early twenties and it just about drove me over the edge. I'm an actor darling, don't you know,' he mocks.

'Well I'm just a nerd,' I say.

'Oh, what sort of nerd?'

'A computer nerd. Into C++ and Java and XML.'

'Sounds exciting.'

'Hardly. But it's the kind of stuff that leads to a good, steady future.'

'Ah, good and steady. Yes, those are the kind of words my wife bandies about when she tries to point out everything I'm not. Well, Olivia, from what I've seen so far, you're also a talented actress.'

'That has yet to be proven.'

'Oh, you'll be fine. Howard's a great guy. He'll look after you.'

I steal a fourth gingernut, dunking it into my tea. Howard pokes his head through the door.

'Ready to roll team?'

We nod and head out into the hall.

The rest of the morning is given up to character development. We are asked to think up mannerisms for our characters, to state their religious inclinations and class, to think about whether or not they are outsiders, whether or not they have any speech impediments, and to think about their deepest secrets and fears. I decide that Charlotte is quite a highly strung, nervous person and that she has a habit of blinking quickly when nervous. She's also very intelligent and craves the approval of others. She is middle class and agnostic. She isn't an outsider; she cares very much about social approval and her friends mean a lot to her. She's a people-pleaser; she wants to be onside with everyone. She had a slight lisp when she was younger, but she went to a speech therapist and overcame it. Her main secret is that she sometimes eats chocolate in bed at night. She's terrified of rats.

Jonathan states that his character, David, is a lapsed Catholic who gesticulates using his hands a lot. David is fiercely competitive and quite ruthless, as he has had to be to get to the top of his profession in the cut-throat music industry. David's biggest fear is being overlooked for promotion and his biggest secret is me, his daughter Charlotte. It's hard work thinking up all this stuff, but quite fun. When we're done with that we rehearse the scene where David first speaks to Charlotte on the phone to tell her that he's her father. Time flies by and before I know it we're eating the catered lunch of chicken sandwiches and samosas and Jonathan and Howard are gossiping about people that they know in 'the industry'.

The afternoon is given over to further work on character development and then it's over for the day. It hasn't gone badly. In fact, I would even venture to say that it's gone quite well.

It's Saturday and I am lying in the lounge going over my lines yet again and writing extensive notes about my character when my twin sister Mel waltzes in through the front door with her boyfriend Quentin in tow.

‘Quentin, could you get me a glass of juice please?’ she bosses.

Quentin trots obediently to the fridge to get her what she asks for.

‘Gosh,’ says Mel. ‘I don’t know why I couldn’t have gotten that myself.’

Quentin smiles weakly. He doesn’t have anything to drink himself. Mel lies back on the La-Z Boy chair while Quentin hovers around her, not taking a seat himself.

‘Hey Quentin,’ says Mel. ‘Could you get me a packet of crisps from the pantry?’

Quentin gets her the packet of crisps.

‘Thanks, darling,’ she says, stuffing her face.

Quentin doesn’t eat anything. I bury myself in my reading.

‘Whatcha up to Livvy?’ asks Mel though a mouthful of crisps.

‘Just going over my lines.’

‘Can’t you have a break? You’re always so into everything, Liv. Into the IT and into the acting. You need to learn to kick back and relax. Like me.’

She takes a swig of her orange juice.

‘Unlike you, Miss Melanie, I take life seriously and try to give my work, whatever it may be, my full attention and effort.’

‘Wah wah wah,’ she says, making a face. ‘Little Miss Perfect.’

I throw down my script in exasperation.

‘Do you mind, Melanie. I’m trying to concentrate.’

‘Concentrate, schmoncentrate. Let’s go out to the pub.’

‘No way. I have work to do.’

She leaps up from her La-Z boy and grabs the script from me.

‘Loosen up baby. Let’s go a-boozing.’

I can see that it’s no use arguing with her.

‘Alright, one. Then I’m getting back to work.’

‘Come on, grab your coat. Let’s go.’

I pick up my coat from where it sits on the back of the sofa and we head across to the Rye. Mel and I walk out in front with Quentin following just behind.

‘Your shout Quentin,’ says Mel, when we get to the bar and Quentin takes out his wallet.

‘It’s okay,’ I say quickly. ‘I can pay for mine.’

‘Oh, I don’t mind,’ he says. ‘I got paid yesterday.’

Quentin works part time at Safeway. He's such a good boy. Mel should be nicer to him, but I suppose that he allows her to treat him in the way that she does. Another guy would tell Mel to get stuffed when she gets all bossy and domineering, but Quentin never seems to. Quentin pays for the beers and we make ourselves cosy on one of the sofas.

'Ah,' says Mel, stretching her legs out. 'It's so great to have the summer to chill out. Quentin and I are going to a beach party on the banks of the beautiful Thames tonight. You wanna come Liv?'

I shake my head.

'Oh, go on. What are you going to do instead? More line-learning?'

'I'm going out with Bev,' I say.

'Oh, good old Bev. At least he smells decent, Livvy, he's not the stinker he used to be. You're training him up well. Men need to be trained, don't they Quentin?'

Quentin says nothing.

'So, what are you up to with old Bevin then?'

'Oh, just the usual. A film at Peckham Multiplex, then dinner at Nando's.'

'Pff,' scoffs Mel. 'Hardly as exciting as a beach party. Why don't you come along with us?'

'No thanks. I've got my own plans.'

'Suit yourself.'

She chugs back half her beer and burps.

'You coming to the Notting Hill Carnival this year Mel? Think of all that jerk chicken.'

'Yeah, thought I might, if Bev wants to go.'

'Oh, you're not turning into one of those girls are you?'

'What girls?'

'Those girls who can't do anything without their boyfriend's say so.'

'No, of course I'm not. Bev and I like to do things as a couple, that's all.'

'Bev'll be into it. Be good for him, get him away from his PC. Mr and Mrs Nerdy hit Notting Hill. Hey Quentin, can you get me another beer? This one's nearly finished.'

Mum upped and left the family last year, left us for her lesbian yoga teacher, a woman called Sue. The relationship lasted all of six weeks and since then Mum's been on her own, flailing through a seemingly endless series of failed love affairs. She never gives up in her search for love. At the moment she's dating Pat, a computer science lecturer at Birkbeck. He's frighteningly clever, an expert in data structures. Mel calls Pat 'Nerdsville Incorporated' but I quite like him, I can relate. For a computer scientist he's got quite good social skills and is always clean and properly shaven.

Mel and I are at Mum's drinking ginger beer and nibbling on crackers and camembert when Mum sees fit to regale us with talk of her latest exploits on the dating front. Mum's on her second glass of wine; I'm starting to get worried about her drinking. She never used to booze when she lived with us. Now she's always with drink in hand.

'Pat and I are taking a holiday in Blackpool,' she says.

'Blackpool?' says Mel. 'Flashing lights, candy floss and general all-round tackiness. Can't you go somewhere a bit more classy?'

'Like where?'

'Oh, Paris, Rome, Prague.'

'Pat's got a fear of flying. We need to keep it local.'

'Surely you can do better than Blackpool.'

'Don't be such a snob, Melanie. I think it'll be very nice. Relaxing to be beside the sea. I need to blow out a bit of stress.'

'And how's work going?' I chime in.

Mum works as an accountant at Simpson and Simpson's in Soho.

'Oh, snowed under as usual. Up to my eyeballs. Harry Simpson sent me home last week, when he emailed me something and I replied straight away and he found I was still in the office at midnight. I mean, he was still working, but he was at home. He told me to go home immediately. Said he didn't want me burning myself out.'

'Well, that's nice. At least they're taking care of you properly. Or attempting to.'

'Oh yes, they're very good. I make rods for my own back really. Always taking on extra work, when some of it could be delegated to colleagues.'

In her personal life, Mum is reckless, ploughing through men (and women, she swings both ways) like there's no tomorrow. In her work-life, she's meticulous, as a good accountant must be. She's extremely hard-working and carries one hell of a load. She hopes to make partner eventually; the Simpsons have told her that it could be on the cards if she keeps up the good work. Then the firm will be Simpson, Simpson and Best; they'll have to change all their business cards, the sign out the front of the building, their letterheads, their email signatures, everything.

'Well, I think Blackpool will be nice, Mum,' I say. 'At least you're getting out of town for a bit.'

'Thank you dear. Exactly.'

Mel scoffs.

'And how are your rehearsals going, Liv?' asks Mum.

'Oh, very well. No complaints so far. The crew all seem very nice.'

'I still can't believe you landed that role,' says Mel. 'You don't know how lucky you are.'

'Your sister is very hard-working,' says Mum. 'I'm sure she'll do a fantastic job.'

'You can only do your best,' I say.

Mum gets up to stir the curry.

'Nearly ready,' she says. 'You girls up for some rogan josh?'

'Oh, yes please,' I say. 'Big plateful for me, all this acting makes me really hungry.'

'Just a little plate for me,' says Mel. 'I'm trying to reduce.'

'Reduce?' says Mum, looking alarmed. 'What do you mean reduce?'

'You know… to lose a bit of weight.

'Oh Melanie,' says Mum. 'I don't want one of my girls becoming like that. Life's hard enough as it is, without trying to get through on minimal calories.'

'I'm getting a fat arse,' says Mel.

'Well, nobody will care about the size of your arse when you're a famous pianist,' counters Mum.

'Ha!' says Melanie. 'That's where you're wrong. People don't want fat hoofers at the piano, they want hot little dollies, easy on the eyes, readily marketable consumer goods.'

'No daughter of mine should think of herself as consumer goods. Piano playing is a talent, a skill. With training you could go a long way. Looks should be irrelevant.'

'Yea, emphasis on the should,' says Mel, signalling that Mum should take a bit of her dinner off her plate and put it back in the pot.

Poetry: Runner-up
J V Birch

Apples and Endings

Stirring from slumber,
my head swims
in green apple dream prints.
Strange, but familiar:
perhaps a prompt for pie-making,
his favourite,
enveloped
in clouds of cream.

Triangles dance on walls
as a sun-catcher teardrop
splinters the light.
They rainbow across
a wine glass of red,
half empty, smeared,
and alone…
He must have left
his downstairs.

I descend to the kitchen
for essentials required:
the door is unusually closed.
A sweet heavy smell
assaults my entrance.
Lilies, on the table,
like silent white screams.
It then hits,
as breath leaves
and the nightmare floods in.
No pudding required.

1st Chapter of a Creative Non-Fiction Book: Runner-up
Ruaidhri Begg

About Donald

We lay beside each other in the dark, a delicious, stomach-wrenching, weightless, anticipatory excitement, recalling childhood Christmas Eves or the day before a long-awaited holiday, spreading through our bodies. I remember a car slipping quietly past the house, its headlights piercing the thin curtains and flashing quickly around the room, picking out badly-applied emulsion and reopened cracks in old walls. Whoever they are, driving home from visiting or the cinema, they don't know why we feel as we do, I thought – why we feel so elated. They don't even know of our existence, lying side by side in one of the many darkened red sandstone houses drawn up like crenellated battlements against a moat of hedged gardens and red granite-chip paths with the straight-as-an-arrow avenue still glistening after a day of rain.

She stirred beside me and took my hand. I squeezed her fingers.

'And what do you want it to be?' she asked.

I thought for a moment. A girl, just like her? I knew she'd like a girl, and I for certain knew her mother would like a girl. Theirs was essentially a family of females striding out of history, generation upon generation, with little or no need of males other than as procreators. Having only a single brother, I knew nothing of girls – certainly not in the role of sibling, so the presence of a new female would be, at least, novel.

Or perhaps it should be a boy? Someone to carry on the name, someone with whom I could share my interests, someone I could find my own father relating to in a way he never related to me. They say that, don't they? Distant fathers becoming all parental and close with the grandchildren. Then I thought of her again, the happy custodian of a tiny life.

'I don't mind,' I said. 'I don't mind what we have as long as it's sound in wind and limb.'

I breathed a sigh of contentment as a distant dog barked away his fear of shadows on what had become a placid, full-moonlit night.

Her even breathing told me that she was sleeping, my words carried away to her dreams.

As long as it's sound in wind and limb....

Nearly three years later, in a different house deep in the country, while our daughter snuffled her way to sleep in the next room, we lay as before, our lives already complete, their paths converged upon a long road of care and upbringing, of work and reward, of a life mapped out full of certainties, without complication, but with more gifts to come.

'And what would you like this time?' she asked.

Once again I thought the same thoughts. But there was a precedent. We had already done right by my family-by-marriage, the granddaughter cum niece dandled endlessly on the knee and handed from proud granny to one aunt after another whenever we went visiting or they came to us, brandishing gifts, seeking baby favours. And I had other ghosts to lay, other obligations to meet. Yes, and my own selfish anticipation of sharing my passions with someone.

'I'd like a boy, this time.'

'Me, too,' she said generously. She stretched and took my hand again, like last time.

A fox cried on the windy and wet moorland beyond the drystane dyke, off in search of young lambs or an unwary farmer's unlocked hen house. Its startled, throttled shriek awakened Morag in the next room – two and a half and never much one for sleeping. My turn to get up.

'Yes,' I said as I pulled on a dressing gown, 'A boy would be awesome'.

This book is a true story masquerading as a work of fiction. As the main characters are all still alive and making their way in the world, their true identities can never be revealed. And it's really of little interest and nobody's business who they are. What matters to you, the reader, is to know and trust that the essentials are true – every last one of them, even though names, locations and the nature of some of the events have been altered to protect the players. And if what this book says about society, the British National Health Service, the Local and Education Authorities, families in general and 'the way it is' hurts and frustrates – well, so be it.

This book, however, is meant to help and to challenge. It is meant to provide people who find themselves in a similar position with some understanding of their predicament and what they might go through and, as a consequence, some hope for the future. And it's meant to make society look at itself, recognise its shortcomings and weep at its lack of compassion and imagination. And it's meant to make those of you who escape the clutches of this particular brand of misfortune eternally grateful. Those must be good things, surely?

What it emphatically is not is a sanitised tome describing, in rounded, glowing phrases, a story of triumph over adversity.

Why?

Because this is not a book of triumph, even though the characters are all still okay after the experience, and Donald – we'll call him Donald – is doing fine at his own level. There can be no real triumph when faced with handicap. Small successes and a dreadful price to pay do not equal triumph. Getting there, but practically being destroyed on the way, is not a success. A complete inability to change the system, so that others will be faced with exactly the same challenges and responses – even from the same individuals – is not an achievement. Proving them all wrong and losing your family in the process does not mean you dwell on easy street.

It must be stated at the outset that this is my story of living with a handicapped person – to be more specific, a mentally handicapped person. It is therefore not Donald's story and it is not even Alex's story. It does not explain how Donald viewed the world and the actions of those closest to him, and it does not give him the opportunity to score his parents' achievements on a scale of one to ten. Donald is, in any case, a man of few words as well as being an extremely private person. Alex, too, will have completely different take on the events of our lives and this is in no way a joint work. I, therefore, do not presume to enter the minds of Donald, Alex, or my daughter Morag for that matter. They all have their 'About Donald' stories.

It will not be an easy read for those of you, poor unfortunates, who are setting out with that same, sickly combination – a dreadful prospect coupled to unfathomable hope. Because, if you are holding on to the straw of a sophisticated, well-provisioned society reaching out to help you – forget it. And if you think you can count on family and friends, forget that too, unless you are exceptionally lucky. It's not like that. As you read this book, you might feel it would be better to look to your own resources for most of what is to come. By all means learn to work the system, but don't actually think they are going to solve things because they are not. In fact, for the most part, they will exacerbate your problems – and that fine word means make it worse. And you may be astounded at the reaction of those closest to you.

Now, this might all sound rather bitter and, I admit it, sometimes I do feel bitter. Bitter at the hand dealt poorly. Bitter at authoritarian ineptitude. Bitter at my own wasted opportunities – things I could have done so much better myself. But, on the whole, it's been worth it. Sure, I'd have liked to have been a part of one of those smug, complacent, middle class couples at parties, bragging gently about Alistair going up to Glasgow to read law, or Kirsty training to be a vet. But then, it was morbidly funny to watch them recoil and seek other company when they asked, innocently, about our two and found that one had a pony and the other was brain damaged and had epilepsy. If their embarrassed curiosity extended to further tentative enquiry, and usually it didn't, oh my goodness, we could talk the hind legs off a donkey! You're supposed to, you see. The Epilepsy Association says so. 'Bring it all into the open,' our local representative said on a crossed-line phone. 'Make people face up to it. Do you know how many people have epilepsy? It's absolutely oodles!' She actually sounded cheerful before asking for our address so we could pay our subscription and join.

We never did, of course.

Donald's epilepsy is not all he has. His epilepsy is downstream from his main problem – the inundated riverside house miles below the breached dam, simply one of the manifestations of his condition. He wouldn't, therefore, be a full member. Rather an odd-ball epileptic, Donald is. Oh, and he doesn't crash out all over the place, melodramatic foaming at the mouth, bladder relaxed unpleasantly and tongue cutting off his air supply if you are really unlucky. I'm telling you that now and you'll probably accept what I say, but if you do, that makes you ahead of the game compared with many of the so-called professionals we had to deal with.

But we brought his epilepsy into the open alright. Told everyone. We had to, because, from an early age, he acted oddly. But that's all rather jumping the gun. I'm into the story before justifying myself and explaining properly that, in spite of it all, I'm not, on the whole, bitter, and certainly not smug, or complacent, or triumphal, or vindictive, or even feeling sorry about my life. It has been hard and sad and difficult at times. But it has been a splendid life – a life in sharp relief; a life experienced and endured and lived to the full – not just a life joined.

Moreover, I feel it is an experience that has to be shared because it's the truth and because it was often lived outside the family, way beyond our four walls. Anyone who has also been on this road will know that, while their experiences may have been different from ours in detail, the general pattern will have been the same. And before it's too late, those of you inescapably treading out along a road with a dimension you never knew existed had better know just how it can be. If you can improve on what I did, and I'm sure you can, you have my endless respect and admiration. Because my story is not one of triumph. But it is real.

Let's start at the beginning when Donald was small. As this is not a biography, we can fast forward from his birth (it was in 1974 by the way) – save to say he was heavy and very late (the doctor did not believe in inducing babies under any circumstances) – and pass all the very earliest stages of babyhood. To all intents and purposes he was a normal baby who was just going to make our family happier, more complete, more complacent and more self-satisfied than ever.

So, what first raised our suspicions that he wasn't quite as he seemed? At precisely what point did the signs – small, subtle, insignificant, but impossible to ignore – begin to penetrate the consciousness and become unexplainable in the conventional sense. When were the indications no longer imagination, no longer just 'perhaps he's tired', no longer 'normal'. Babies are not all the same. In fact, none of them are the same. They are as distinctive, unique and curious as adults. So, it takes a long time to make any distinction between normal and abnormal behaviour. And then, of course, it takes a long time to admit the presence of that abnormal behaviour.

Most mornings I used to lift him from his cot – a warm blue Babygro with a sleepy head and uncoordinated hands at one end, and an eye-watering, chlorine smell emanating from somewhere around the middle. A quick change (followed frequently by a repeat performance – why do babies do that?) and he was down to his high-chair in the kitchen where he would rub his eyes and wait contentedly while I warmed his jar of unrecognisable breakfast cereal. I swear the labels on those jars are purely for adult consumption – delightfully descriptive, full of variety, comfortingly familiar – 'pureed cereal with apple', the label would coo, 'a delicious start to your baby's day'.

What they are like now, I don't know, but in the seventies the contents had the consistency of an over-wet Polyfilla mix, the colour was indistinguishable from puke and they smelled of nothing at all.

But Donald was content. Donald was always content. While, at the same age, Morag would rattle the bars of her cot and howl the place down if everything was not just so, Donald was content to stare around him placidly. He was often awake in his cot, just laying there, his face wreathed in smiles when I went into his room, threw back the curtains and jiggled his mobile into life. In the highchair, while I struggled with the lid of the jar and plopped it into a pan of warm water, he would watch me closely but seemed content to wait for ever, so long as there was something to distract him. He was, in short, the ideal baby. And he was so beautiful! Blonde curls that might last forever – imitating his mother, a round face forever grinning, and a chortling laugh that made everyone smile.

But why did the smile leave his face mid-mouthful and his head rock back and forth for a second or two? Was he, perhaps, not sitting up straight? Or was the highchair just a bit too large for him? It was quite big, one of those odd, cumbersome, wooden beasts that had wheels that didn't touch the ground and extraneous components to make it into something else. Perhaps the baby rocker might be a better breakfasting bet – one of those angled frames with stretched canvas that sit on the floor? But that's why it wasn't a good solution. Even in my twenties, bending down to within eight inches of the floor to spoon mush into my son would have been difficult. No, the highchair won the day. But then, there was Donald's rocking motion.

Looking back, it was quite attractive, really. Momentary, quickly recovered from, distinctive. My first reaction, after I'd unsuccessfully tried wedging cushions around the seat to stop him from wobbling, was to tell him off – rather as I did the cat when, displeased with its breakfast, it tried to turn the plate over.

'Don't do that, Donald,' I'd say, 'this is really lovely food! Mmm! Look! Daddy's just at the point of eating your lovely breakfast himself!'

Having children makes liars of us all.

Donald would display his wide grin, repeatedly smack the surface of the tray in pleasure at my antics (and, probably, my insincerity) and obediently take another mouthful. And just as the last scrapings from the spoon disappeared into his toothless mouth and I thought only one little nod during the entire meal was pretty good – probably just a wee habit of his – he would do it again.

During the day, the events became less noticeable. Perhaps that was simply because we were busy. As an architect, at that time I worked largely from home. My wife was a district nurse working part-time, in and out and nicely co-ordinated around my frequent visits to clients. And, anyway, he was always crawling away and, presumably, having a wee absence whenever he was bored. We kidded ourselves it was just a breakfast thing – some little habit he'd grow out of.

As I had seen the phenomenon most frequently, due to our household routine, we agreed I would make an appointment at the surgery. So, at the appointed time, plus an hour or so spent in the waiting room, I told the doctor about it and he screwed up his mouth and put down the prescription pad he was dying to use. He could do eczema, croup and inflamed gums without thinking, but this required lip-pursing thought.

'Hmmm,' he said, as doctors do, 'can you describe it again?'

I did.

More mastication.

'Well, he looks well enough. Is he eating well? Sleeping well? Progressing normally?'

Yes to all.

'Well,' he said, slapping his expensive pen down on the desk and lifting his stethoscope, 'I'll give him the once over but he'll probably grow out of it.'

It's great to have your own theories confirmed.

The doctor whistled through his teeth as he tapped and poked and prodded and nodded to himself with considerable self-satisfaction. I have noticed we are often our own greatest admirers.

'Baby's heads are heavy,' he said. I wondered if he was talking to me or simply reminding himself of a self-evident fact.

'Are they?' I responded stupidly.

'Oh, yes, can be, oh… I can't remember… what… at this age? Can be a third of their body weight – more.'

'Really?' Since Donald's head was getting on for a third of his body length, it seemed about par for the course and in no way surprising. But, then, I am not an expert.

'Could be just that his neck-muscles are not fully developed. Seems okay in all other respects. New parents can get extremely anxious, you know. Especially your class, if you know what I mean.

The Lord protect us from thrusting professionals, eh? Always trying to turn their kids into brain surgeons before they can walk!' He smiled.

I was not particularly amused.

Short Story: Runner-up
Sarah Crossland

How to Date the Girl with the Middle-Parted Hair

1.*On Recognizing What You've Always Wanted*
It takes something like sugar-free gum. She asks you, while you are driving her to buy flour because her car is in the shop, for a piece of gum. You make a joke about her breath, and if it were anyone else, you would get cocky and stroke her leg, or touch her hair, because she looks so good in that red sweater, and it's almost impossible that she's wearing a bra. Instead, you don't ignore what she said, and you check to see what gum you have. It's Cinnamon Trident, and you only have one piece left. You don't even think about your own breath, you don't dream of kissing her madly on the lips against the driving wheel, at a stop light, even though this particular stop light seems to last forever. Instead, you give her your last piece of gum. And it is all of these *insteads* that makes you realize.

2. *On Who to Be*
She is certain she adores poets who don't shave. Also, young men fascinated with fire-fighting, though not actually willing to go into training for the job. She finds something sexy about this obscure cowardice, this passionate desire for unbridled hotness, for the feel of limp and then erect hoses igniting townhouses with their lantern-streams of water. She is aware that she wants paradoxes, but they are the most important thing. Tight sweaters or jeans, badly-laced sneakers, Paul McCartney-length hair at the time that *Help!* was released. Most importantly, though, there is a need for men who are well-acquainted with tying knots. 'The half-hitch,' she imagines saying to her lover, as they sit naked and cross-legged in front of a fire, she playing with his hair, and he leaning over, ruining his spine even more, as she thinks *No no that's a bowline,* and imagines a hook and a fish, a trout, shining pink and green as it floats a foot up in the air. After she tells you all this, you go home and try writing poetry.

3. *On Daily Interactions and Existing With Her, Too*
You know that you are none of these things, but you know that you can still be friends, as always, and maybe will get something perfect

from it some day: a drunken blow job, or a carefully-made scrapbook, with small blue paper frames (whichever way your friendship, eventually, turns). At first, you live in the apartment above hers, and dream of the floor melting like butter or Fontina cheese, of collapsing right into her arms as she lies half on the couch, half off, watching a midnight special featuring Clark Gable and Marilyn Monroe. And then when there is a vacancy, you move across the street (to a lower rent, yes, and a dishwasher, you reason), and call her when you want to go get bagels. It's a maddening thing, watching her from across the street, as she buttons her grey pea coat, and slips her gloves on. *It's like what sex will be*, you think. *The gloves and I. It will be the grandest movement in the world.*

4. *On Thinking of Approaching Her, Or Building Skyscrapers Out of Your Love*

The thing to remember is, she understands that you love her. She has known this since you were both in the second grade, and during her first piano recital, when you clapped loudly at the coda. Afterwards, you brought her pink and brown tea cookies on a crumpled napkin, and urged her to eat up your love. She asked for punch. You brought it. Or, there is the possibility that she knew later, when you happened to sit next to each other during Geography class because your names came one after the other in alphabetical order. She knew when you asked for help in labelling the countries in Africa, or just barely after. 'Angola,' you said, 'that sounds kind of like your name.' 'What?' she laughed, 'it sounds nothing like it.' And you smiled, and it was then, right then, that she realized. You see, she's known for years, or decades.

5. *On Saying What You Mean*

Once, while she was dating a blonde soccer player, in high school, they stood outside an English classroom after receiving their graded papers on *The Tempest*. It was only a few days into their relationship, and the boy said, 'No hickies, that's something I wanted to say.' And the girl looked at him, her eyes the colour of raspberries, of bruised skin, of pictures of the sun, and she said, 'I don't think we should have sex, either.' Two years later, as the two reminisced (after meeting coincidentally in the park), both sipping the same drink of tonic water teased with lime, the boy said, 'Remember what I told you outside Miss Keaton's room?' The girl nodded her head, and the boy said, 'I wanted sex more than anything,' and the girl said, 'So did I.' She tells you this story, after high school, after college, one night after you've been out dancing – with other people. You laugh awkwardly, because you remember this boy. He got higher grades than you in chemistry. You dated his sister and dumped her, twice. But more importantly, he – if only for a moment – won the love of this girl with the middle-parted hair.

6. *On Doing Nothing*

She falls asleep one time, at your apartment. You've been watching *Cleopatra* because she's obsessed with Elizabeth Taylor and the possibility of violet eyes. Her hair is a mess on her head, her part something like a line in sand disturbed by wind – or the fan buzzing loudly overhead. When she wakes up, the credits are up to Gaffer and Key Grip, and you are sucking on the popcorn kernels that she has left at the bottom of the bowl. Smiling stupidly, you sit there and do nothing; or, you sit and smile stupidly at the wrinkled skin that's begun collecting at the corners of her eyes, or the places where her mascara has copied itself onto her cheeks. Like the art projects from pre-school, where you pour pools of red and blue paint on paper, and fold it, and somehow, when the inside is hidden from the world, the ugly purple mess becomes art.

7. *On Trying to Make Her Jealous with the Blonde Girl from Your Gym*

One day, while at the gym with your cousin, you tell him everything. After you have explained your burning desire to touch your hand to her upper back, or to share a cone of chocolate ice cream, he says plainly, 'You should just sleep with her.' 'You don't under*stand*,' you say, with exquisite emphasis, 'things can't happen like that.' 'No,' he says, 'I mean *her*.' He's pointing to a blonde girl in grey sweat pants and a hot pink sports bra. She looks as if her name could be Mindy, or Faith. She smiles as she walks up to you; it's not like you haven't done this before, to get away. 'A little vacation,' he says. 'It's like Acapulco, or Guam.' 'Guam?' you say. 'No one goes to Guam for their vacation.' But you end up inviting the girl out for coffee, which becomes an Asian salad, and then finally expensive steak. When you get back to your apartment, you fall asleep with the lights on, in your socks, with her number bleeding blue ink on your hand.

8. *On Informing the Girl with the Middle-Parted Hair That You Are In Fact Sleeping with Someone Else*

You call her up, one Saturday afternoon, to tell her that you've met a girl, her name is Cindy, and she is interested in cartography. Instead, you inadvertently start a fight over whether or not blueberries are in season. She mentions something about the new grocery store that's opened up, and how fresh the blueberries are this year, and you can't stop yourself from saying, 'But blueberries aren't in season yet, you know.' She insists that you're wrong, that she read this recipe in *Good Housekeeping* for a cobbler and remarked on the timing of the grocery store's ad. You tell her that you know your fruit, you know your calendar, your grandfather was a farmer. You remind her that *her* grandfather was in politics, and she huffs at this, as if we can all be defined by the smoky blue eyes and the weighty, branch-like hands of our grandfathers. After hanging up the phone three minutes later, you hope that she'll find out you're dating this girl through a friend of a friend, or at the dry cleaners'. She's always listening in on what people are saying at the dry cleaners'. Instead you find out that she's dating a chef named Lawrence. These insteads are still piling on; it makes realizing sharper; it makes it happen every second.

9. *On Receiving a Phone Call in the Middle of the Night, About Technology*

Your girlfriend insists on sleeping naked, even though you've told her about the risk of burglars. Also: forest fires. So when you receive a call at four in the morning, and throw back the covers to unplug your cell phone from its charger, she moans about the draft coming from the open window, and falls back asleep. Because you wear contacts, you cannot see what the Caller ID reads. 'Yes,' you say mildly into the phone, taking the call into the living room. 'Can I *help* you?' You sit down on the sofa. 'It's me,' she says – the girl who parts her hair right down the middle. 'My DVD player is broken. I was in the middle of *A Place in the Sun* and it just stopped.' 'Is that the one with Montgomery Clift?' you say. 'He's such a great actor.' 'He's gay,' she says, as if somehow you will find this discrediting, even though you saw *Brokeback Mountain* in theatres, and have four good friends who are gay. 'I thought you were gay when we first met,' she says. 'Have I told you that before?' 'You think everybody's gay.' 'Half the time I'm right.' You go on to discuss the nature of clothes pins, and the meaning of chlorine when used outside public pools. Eventually: men.

'They're just such *vagabonds*,' she says. You smile, and without hanging up, fall fast asleep.

10. *On Inadvertently Telling Your Girlfriend to Be Someone Else, Namely The Girl with the Middle-Parted Hair*
'You could be a brunette,' you tell your girlfriend over Shrimp Gabriella. 'It would match your facial structure. Your bones, I mean. And your skin.' She is obviously offended by the fact that you don't love her almost-white hair. She begins to pull it back more often, or wear headbands. You suggested this, too, but she was more obliging with these things, because after all, she really loves you. Another thing, though, that upsets her is what you've done to her idea of music. 'You should listen to these bands,' you tell her, 'I know you'll love them.' But she doesn't like looking up words in dictionaries while trying to sound out syllables in between bell solos, and she doesn't understand the allusions to photosynthesis, or the human bone structure. 'I wasn't a biology major,' she pleads with you. You look at her – you're in bed, wrapped up in the light from a single desk lamp and sheets the colour of her eyes – and you say quietly, 'I wasn't either.'

11. *On Refrigerators*
Every time you see a refrigerator, you are reminded of the girl with the middle-parted hair. She happens to love refrigerators. Also: tape dispensers and anything the colour of cheddar cheese. But not: paper weights. They make her uncomfortable.

12. *On the Accidental Swapping of Lingerie, Which Your Girlfriend Assures You Can Be No Accident*
You and the girl with the middle-parted hair have done your laundry together for years. It's a strange bonding thing that began when you came to class wearing light pink socks. So when you come home with a dark red bra that is not your girlfriend's, you're not entirely surprised. After all, it's happened before: the green polo shirt she bought at that thrift store in Maine, a long black skirt from The Limited that she always swears she's never worn. (She just washes it because she can't stand the thought that, maybe, it's become dirty from unuse.) 'This *isn't* mine!' your girlfriend screams, throwing it at the lamp you can turn on just by touching it. It hangs there, momentarily, before collapsing on the carpet. Instead of telling the

truth, you tell her you're having an affair with an older woman from your parents' yacht club. 'Her name is Barbara,' you lie. 'She's into poodles. But you'd like her a lot, I think.'

13. *On Doing Nothing*
One time, when you were both in middle school, with teeth that shined bright railroad tracks of braces, fingers that piped hotly – madly – to the beat of loud and rearranged dance hits, you knew that she was in love with this boy that she was seeing, named Carl. It was terrible because he also played the saxophone and went to Earth Club. At the time, you thought She's going to sleep with him, she's going to do it, because Carl was the type of boy who fucked virgins instead of learning his Pre-Algebra. But she didn't sleep with him, or the next fourteen boys she let take her out for strawberry shakes, or French fries fried in peanut oil. She slept with a guy named Tucker. She was twenty, and sober. You let her tell you about him one night shortly after it's happened, you let her interrupt your game of Scrabble. And then you beat her with the word 'despatch.' 'That's not a real word,' she protested. 'It's with an i.' 'No,' you said, 'it is, and it means the same thing.'

14. *On Doing Nothing*
It has been a month since your girl friend left you, and you have only seen the girl with the middle-parted hair four times. Allegedly, it is because she has a new case, something with spotted ducks in Canada, and you've of course upgraded your gym pass which consumes every minute of spare time. But still, it is something you count – how many times you see her. You've always counted. You count the blue birds you see as you walk to work (Eastern Blue Birds, Blue Birds of Paradise). You count how many seconds it takes for her to answer the phone when you call. Or, you count how often it snows, how often you check the window to see how much it's snowing. If it's snowing outside, you will not be aware of it, though, because you are thinking of how snow-like her skin is. On her elbows, her palms, at the very corners of her eyes.

15. *On the Future, Or: What Happens Next*
Years later, you will be sitting here – an old desk your father made from three slats of wood, or at that coffee bar that sells more cupcakes than it does coffee – and you will be thinking how it could possibly

mean something: the elbows, the jelly sandwiches, the way she only smiles partway, or the way she lets her cheeks grow raw in winter. The thing is, you're moving to Buffalo. You're okay with Buffalo, and while you're convincing yourself that you are, in fact, okay with Buffalo, you instead write a nineteen page poem about her hair: its straight brown quilting, and how it parts so perfectly, in the middle. You imagine a year later, when you surely will run into her again – downtown, at a video store of all places – and she'll ask, 'How are you doing?' – she's here on business – and you'll say that you are well, but really you will mean, I have written you a poem and I pretend that it doesn't exist. She will say, 'Remember the Halloween we dressed up as Dan Aykroyd and Donna Dixon?' *Of course*, you will think, *that's when you kissed me and I didn't kiss back.* But instead you will say, 'Junior year of high school. Right?' 'I don't know,' she will say, 'if it was the sunglasses, or me wearing that wig, but I'm sorry for that, I know it – ' But she will stop, and laugh, and you will too – hands numb, lips frozen (because after all, it is December) – and you will realize that you should have learned years and years ago how to date the girl with the middle parted hair, how to break a statue, or what it would mean to even try. You realize, you could have done it then. Only now, it's impossible.

Poetry: Runner-up

Juliet O'Callaghan

Under the Wig

The wooden rail is cold -
And my fingers seem to stick
Like the words under my tongue
And the sperm you made me lick.

The Jury does not smile
As the judge reads out your plea,
And the Jury does not cry
At what you did to me.

My words are diced
Chopped and fried.

Your lies are spliced
Cut and dried.

So, said wig sheep
She was on the pull?

Yes sir, yes sir
Consent was full

Yay! when I asked her,
Oh no, when I came,
And here I am a good boy
Trapped in this slut's game.

Creative Non-fiction Essay: Runner-up

Desmond Meiring

Pride and a Fall

Four days before the end of the safari I still had not got Barry Johnson his lion. Five days earlier, I had brought us back to Negoti, near our first camp where Johnson had killed his buffalo just before it killed us. I had even engaged a local lion-guide called Mchege. He was elderly and felt-hatted. We chased his intuitions and local rumour and one or two-day-old spoor. Yet there was one pride and perhaps two about; we heard them at night. I started to hear satire in their roars. But I counselled myself patience. Here, a lion usually spent his life in an area of about 30 by 30 miles unless the drought was bad or he was chased out. We must find one, in time. But that was what we lacked. Johnson had asked if I would prolong the trip. I had been evasive. A little Barry Johnson went a long way.

That dawn was the second we had been to the bait of two wildebeest we had set up in a tall tree, in bush by a salt lick by the river. But hyena had bust through the thorn and dragged off the wildebeest on the ground and eaten nearly all of it, and most of the chest and forelegs of the wildebeest hanging from the tree. Mchege showed us where lion had looked at the bait in the night. There was spoor of what looked like a big male and two females but they must already have killed and fed. I told my gun-bearers Kolokolo and Juma and Mutiso the Kamba skinner to cut down the top wildebeest to recover my rope. We left, depressed.

To distract my clients I drove back a different route, practically letting the Land Rover find its own way. After a mile we saw the lion. He had evaded us all that month as if by magic. Here at last was the archetype of history, 5,000-year-old motif on the Cylinder of Suse, sculpted companion of the Priestesses of Nineveh, guardian in stone of the Royal Terrace at Angkor Wat, trained hunter for the Assyrians 1,000 years before Christ. After that month's bitter search it was like finding a god.

We had come upon him round a patch of bush lifting to a rise, behind which the sun's first rays flared. At once I eased the car to a stop and cut the motor. The lion stood at the top of the rise in profile, silhouetted against that golden blaze. He was very fine, full-grown, seven or eight years old, sheer tawny, no black. He stood still and watched the Land Rover with his tranquil, timeless cat's eyes. If you were close enough, you would see splinters of darker gold flecking the wide gold irises. The lion was simply curious. He did not move even the end of his low tufted tail, nor any of the heavy powerful muscles of his shoulders and chest and the smoother flank muscles. When he advanced they would flow together into that rippling stride that was all luxuriance, yet also balance and control and economy. He had chosen his moment dramatically, etched out against that dawn sky, fired with stronger upward rays now, mounting gold upon gold to the high light-blue heavens.

I kept my eyes on the lion all the time, and put my arm round slowly for the Holland and Holland four-seventies. I doubted that the lion would see that movement. The Land Rover was pointed head-on to him. By now the sunlight must be on the windscreen and reflecting from it, masking all behind it. To the lion, the car would have been simply a large squat thing with ridiculously short legs and a revolting smell. No animal in its right mind would go anywhere near it let alone try to eat it. At least it seemed harmless, just watching with its one monstrous blinding oblong eye.

Kolokolo passed us the four-seventies forward, and Johnson and I broke them quietly and loaded each with its two thick long soft-nosed cartridges. The lion still had not moved. I said softly to Johnson: 'Make it 20, 30 yards from the car. The shoulder or just behind. Low if he charges, not the head. Remember the safety!' He slid out.

'Can I go too?' whispered his wife Carolyn, still elegant in her wide-brimmed hat with its anti-gnat veil, avid as ever with her camcorder. I replied as low-pitched: 'No. Please stay in the car. Best shot's from here anyway. I go only to cover him.'

I slid out too. Johnson was now some 40 to 50 yards out, crouched, moving slightly forward so as not to increase his distance from the lion. He had his head twisted towards him all the time, as if trying to hold him there by sheer willpower. The lion was taking a good deal more interest in him too. He was twitching his splendid head slowly from Johnson to the Land Rover and back again, as if puzzled by this sudden and abnormal birth. I thought, he'll go! Christ, he'll go! I looked back in dreadful suspense at Johnson and saw his four-seventy come up slowly and easily and go rock steady. I heard its quick heavy roar as I looked back at the lion. He had bunched himself low like lightning in the precise instant that Johnson shot, doubtless to go into a charge. I felt in my guts the incredible shock in that bunched coiled body, and knew that Johnson had certainly hit him.

The lion moved forward very slowly. His gold eyes were narrowed and his nose puckered up. His mouth was opened now in those deep prolonged back-of-the-throat growls that pierced right through you and shivered you under your fingernails, however often you had heard them. The lion's eyes were set on Johnson and he dragged himself steadily towards him with obvious enormous effort. I saw that he was pressing his hind legs together as if to hold in terrible pain, in his kidneys or high in his loins. Hit him again, you bastard, I said mentally to Johnson – the *shoulders*! Hit him *again*! And I had raised my own four-seventy already and sighted down the shotgun vee between the twin barrels when I heard Johnson's second shot and saw the lion go down. I said curtly: 'Reload before you go forward!' and watched Johnson eject and put in two fresh cartridges from the stitched line above his pockets.

We went together to the lion. I said: 'Not too near. You can't tell yet.' We stood a moment with our four-seventies and looked down at him. He was on the ground now, but not on his side. Bright blood came from his nose and mouth. We saw the two small holes in his left side, one far back as I had thought, and high, the other a little behind his shoulder. We heard the tearing sounds as his claws extended fully and bit into the ground under him, again and again. The deep rolling gutturals still came from his throat and his magnificent gold cat's eyes still looked straight through us. His body was dying and that was all.

'My God, he's beautiful!' said Carolyn ecstatically from just behind us, and we heard the shutter of her camera click.

'You shouldn't really be here yet,' I said severely.

'Oh, let her stay,' exclaimed Johnson, not at all averse to an expanded audience. I shrugged. It was his safari and his wife. I had done my little bit, following that old adage that a white hunter was judged on the big game he got killed and the clients he did not.

Kolokol, ever the perfect gun bearer anticipating all needs, had pitched up with Johnson's 30.06. I said: 'A little to one side. By the ear.' Johnson moved in and lifted the 30.06 up to his shoulder. Right on top of the lion, he seemed to be leaning on it with the rifle. They could have been cut out statuesque for all the time like that, the lion's great head up towards him and the eyes always watching him.

The rifle gave its high small-bore crack and the body rolled over obediently. The lion lay still and gave a deep sigh.

Enormously relieved, I looked at Johnson. 'Well,' I said, 'That's about it.'

Johnson actually smiled.

'You didn't shoot?'

'No.'

I looked around suddenly. The first vultures had arrived. Two sat already in the thorn tree next to which the lion had been standing when we first saw him. As we watched, more planed down and perched and ringed us politely. They sat so still that within seconds they appeared to have been there permanently, like obscene fruits. I looked up and saw more gathering, jagged-edged black wings swinging in the clear blue sky.

Johnson looked back at his lion. He said: 'Curious way they look right through you.'

'You can't kill that,' I replied. 'You can't nail that up on a wall.'

'No,' said Johnson, not sounding convinced.

'You've got a damned good one,' I went on encouragingly. 'It's what you wanted, right?'

'Sure,' said Johnson.

'They don't come much better,' I continued.

That was true enough. His lion was near perfect. The head and mane were very fine, and he had no bad scars on his hide. He was about nine foot six from the tip of his nose to the end of his tail, and he would weigh 370 to 400 pounds.

Johnson stirred the lion with his foot.

'After all that trouble,' he said, 'it suddenly seemed so easy.'

'Perhaps too easy,' I said.

'Maybe if I tried it completely alone,' Johnson suggested.

'No reason why you shouldn't,' I replied. 'Some day.'

Not on one of my trips, though, I thought. Johnson was dangerous because he would never really be satisfied. He would always want too much.

'What's this character up to, Desmond?' asked Carolyn, who had just finished her first spool on the lion and us from every angle.

This character was my second gun bearer Juma, who was a natural clown. He and the elderly local guide Mchege were looking ostentatiously at the grass around the dead lion's head. I laughed. 'It's one of the local stunts. An old myth that the lion carries a ball of hair in his stomach and throws it up when he dies. It's supposed to be stuffed with magic. Very popular with the *waganga*, witch-doctors.'

'I don't believe in that sort of crap,' said Johnson disdainfully.

Juma, the born comic, recognised the imperious tone at once, and cast around for fresh material. What better than the elderly guide, Mchege, right next to him? Hands on his hips before him, Juma began to chant in Kiswahili, which I translated for Johnson and Carolyn:

Oh, what a fine hunter is Mchege,
Who really finds nothing at all,
An old man already frightened by life,
An old man who cannot find what he looks for,
Who looks for the wrong things in the wrong place,
His eyes clouded by dreams,
Who can no longer succeed at things!

'Your gun bearer wouldn't be aiming at me, by any chance?' asked Barry Johnson in steely tone. 'Looking for the wrong things in the wrong places, for example?'

I looked at him, genuinely startled. Such an interpretation had never even occurred to me, until now. We were both distracted by Mutiso the Kamba skinner, who had joined forces vigorously with Juma. 'Indeed!' he said aggressively. 'What sort of guide *are* you, Mchege? Who for the four days here say to us every day: "I'll find you lion today!" then: "Oh, tomorrow I'll certainly find you lion!" and then: "It's this way, Bwana!" or "It's that way, Bwana!"'

Juma came in neatly on the blank verse beat, neat as a dancer: 'And when we find what we seek, O Mchege, who finds it? You? No, *we* find it. And it was there all the time.'

The two gun bearers had joined in, nodding too sagely in judgement. Then Juma delivered his most telling indictment: 'Furthermore, one sees that his hat is old and has many holes.'

The four Africans watched him. Mchege took off his hat and examined it in great misery.

'That is true. That is all true.'

'Nonetheless,' I broke in, feeling that the underdog deserved some sort of relief, 'let's accept that Mchege did his best. He thought he was finding the lion. He tried to search for something great.'

That ought to cover friend Barry Johnson too, I thought.

‘And now let’s skin this damned lion,’ I went on crisply in English, and motioned to Mutiso. The skinner beamed to show he had understood. That revealed his splendidly filed upper teeth.

‘Alright, teeth-as-fierce-as-a-lion’s. Put them away now.’

Kolokolo and Juma took off and set aside their clean starched bush-jackets, and held the lion’s body for the skinner’s knife. Mutiso slit down the centre of the belly and up inside the legs, and they helped him pull the skin away. It was as if they ungloved the lion carefully. They took the paws and head intact, rolled up the skin and took it to the car, the still connected head over Kolokolo’s shoulder.

Johnson and I gazed down at the naked truncated body. The intricate black veins and arteries ran like rivers under the skin. Nerves still twitched in the sheathed bunches of muscles. To have reduced that power and grace to this seemed a desecration.

‘So, what happens next?’ asked Johnson, clearly not too profoundly moved, still keen to get full value for his money.

‘Oh, well, your triumphant return to camp…’

That involved us cutting down plenty of branches and dolling up the Land Rover to make it obvious to one and all in the camp that Johnson had at last achieved his great aim of killing a lion. That would include giving tips all round too to the Africans with us and those in the camp, and hearty shouts and singing at our arrival. But there was no such furore yet. Instead, the fine African game was spread out tranquilly, hardly bothering to notice us passing. We saw splendid herds of Thomson’s and Grant’s Gazelle, sprayed out gracious as rain, kongoni, zebra, devil-bearded and humped wildebeest, a few eland and solitary giraffe, and impala who put on their epic parabolic leaps for us, as if in slow motion through clear water.

And the lioness. I braked the Land Rover gently and stopped. The lioness lay statuesque, facing us, a belt of thick brush behind her, her gold cat’s eyes fathomless. A two-month-old cub gambolled by her. She glanced at it and lay down. Carolyn peeked out with her camera from the back seat. The lioness must have seen that. She got up, her cub echoing her, and stood regally, fine grave head motionless, ears pricked at us, the intruders. The tip of her tail flicked very slightly, but with all the impact of a raised ministerial eyebrow.

‘Should I shoot her?’ asked Barry Johnson.

He truly appalled me. ‘No. No, you’d hardly want that skin.’

I looked at the lioness. Such sudden sights justified my whole life. For I’d always hunted far more for Kenya’s beauty than for the trophies. I had my rewards. No man can know a land so well, in its dawns and nights, heats and colds, grandeurs and utter furies, in all its textures, as can the hunter.

So with huge secret laughter I watched the lioness nudge her cub now. It trotted off obediently into the thick bush. She followed, long smooth muscles rippling exquisitely. She took her time. No one should imagine they were pushing her out.

The African bush reacted subtly. Barry Johnson had now shot everything on his licence, so we drank more than usual at our extra-large lunch, then slept it off in our tents. Carolyn, distraught, called me at 6pm. Barry had woken her up at 4pm to say he'd walk for an hour – no, he'd not bother with a firearm, for the bush was really hardly any more dangerous than a fairly large park, was it? People just exaggerated.

Not this time, though. From 5pm Carolyn had suffered agonies. She was already convinced of the worst. I took her and my two gun bearers in the Land Rover at once. I guessed that Barry had gone across the dried river bed into the vast forest area beyond. The danger there was that you could only see the encircling tall trees and bush, no convenient orienting mountains. I'd got lost in such bush once, and knew the utter terror it provoked, the dreadful conviction that you walked or ran endlessly in deadly circles, shadowed by mocking predators, a malignant intelligence that painted all faint paths alike. Now we stopped regularly and fired a shot, to guide Barry. I'd been rescued because I answered with my rifle, but Barry had scorned carrying one. We found him at 9pm, as the perilous night fell, collapsed, exhausted. Thorns had ripped his clothes and skin, and he wept. We dosed him heavily with brandy and got him back fast to bed. He was a quiet man when we drove him to Nairobi next morning.

Hunting can teach you. I think Barry learned. He was a good straightforward guy at heart. And I'm sure that that lioness would long ago have forgiven him his lethal intent towards her.

1st Chapter of a Creative Non-Fiction Book: Runner-up
Marilyn Messenger

Man of Stars

I read other people's letters just as surely as if I were at their shoulder as the ink flowed or there when the brittle seal snapped and the letter slipped from the envelope.

> *My dear Miss Earle, I have not yet done myself the pleasure of thanking you for your very kind letter of the 13th ult., in which you gave me an account of your efforts to recover poor Tippoo, or to learn something certain respecting him...*

As an opening sentence, this had everything necessary to reel me in and soon I was so absorbed that the writer, across more than 140 years, must have felt the whisper of my breath prickle the hair on their neck; making them pause and glance about the room inquiringly.

I turned the folded paper to where the letter was signed, *Remain, my dear Miss Earle, your faithful friend W R Dawes,* in lettering that arched and coiled from one character to the next and concluded with an underscore of the surname – not as a flourish, more a decisive stroke of the pen.

A rustle of parchment and a waft of elderly dust returned me to the 21st century and the cool of a Cumbrian auction room where long wooden tables held cardboard boxes crammed with bundles of documents: deeds, indentures and letters. The sooty contents of solicitors' attic storerooms, fragile fragments of lives lived, disputes settled and wills scribed were piled in unseemly heaps. The neat packet of letters I picked up was small and intriguing.

Handling the past can feel intrusive. If they could see what has become of their private documents, these long dead people, would they care? Would the dry shuffle of paper become a low murmuring of voices raised in protest? I sensed the disapproval of solicitors hunched over large oak desks, and that of their clerks who scratched a living across the crackle and fold of parchment. Victorian landowners with double Albert watch chains looped in a declaration of prosperity and self-assurance would bluster at the indignity of the scene.

The numbers of those who hunt the past continues to grow. Record offices fill with amateur genealogists seeking information about their ancestors and perhaps about themselves. Files fill with dates of births, marriages and deaths which form the roots and branches of family trees. Faded photographs are particularly treasured, and scanned for characteristics which may have been inherited by the face they see in their mirror. To have a letter written by the ancestor who sits stiffly in a sepia photograph; that is to see the tree blossom.

Genealogical information is available from many sources and is diverse and vast. David Annal, a member of staff at The National Archives in Kew, is an expert on census returns and author of 'Census: The Expert Guide'. In a talk he gives about using the newly released 1911 Census, Annal likes to mention the Moulting family who, much as the last dodos, were the only remaining family members with this surname – they had no children. After giving his audience this poignant fact he pauses in the hopeful expectation that, one day, someone will call out indignantly that he is wrong and that their neighbour or local greengrocer bears the name Moulting.

There's an ache in the desire to discover your lineage, in the collecting of names which often concludes with such a biblical begetting that your own name appears feeble on an *Yggdrasil* of a family tree that must surely be felled under the colossal weight of ancestors.

I came to realise that the people whose letters I read need have no connection to me at all. I still crave their words, still need to identify them – when and where they lived, what was happening in their world – regardless of any genetic link. Were their thoughts and feelings at all different to ours; were they happy, healthy, did they love and hate, make promises and break them? I acquire these fragments of the past through private letters and I try to glean answers. There's something of the treasure hunt in this – not knowing what might be hidden in script that is often difficult to read at first glance.

I observed the other would be bidders. All were men, and alike in their ways as they moved meticulously from table to table. Some peered over bifocal spectacles and made cramped observations in small notebooks, almost furtively. Others were probably dealers browsing acres of parchment in search of a profit, a few were perhaps looking to add to their private collection of documents.

If any of them harboured any enthusiasm for a particular lot then, like poker players, they hid it well behind impassive expressions and lack of eye contact. The letters I am attracted to could be described as 'chatty' or 'familiar' and from a quick glance at the letters I held in my hand, they appeared to fit that description.

The art of letter writing has been examined critically from the time of Cicero to the present day and many academics have given their views on epistolary writing. None of them, I think, would have thought highly of the letters that I enjoy.

William Roberts wrote a weighty book about the history of letter writing and, as a barrister, he was no doubt used to pontificating in the courtroom so his book required in excess of 700 pages to reach the fifth century. I did find one paragraph that I could relate to, in the dedication. Not for Roberts were there a couple of lines dedicating the book to his wife perhaps (who bore him ten children) but instead, a ten page 'Epistle Dedicatory' to his brother-in-law, Alexander Radclyffe Sidebottom Esq. Roberts (1843) advises that:

> *The play of a letter should be natural, its wit unconscious, and its vigour involuntary. In a real (sic) good letter there should be something vital, something belonging to the interior man, as he stands affected by passing events, or his own experiences and recollections.*

A very large nutshell would be needed for a précis of Roberts's dedication, but in the above paragraph he has captured the reasons why I enjoy reading letters and what I hope to find in them.

I bought the small package of letters and I wish that I could describe the triumph of the auctioneer's hammer descending at my successful bid; my heart thumping as the price rose – but the tension of an auction is too taut for me. Cowardly, I left a maximum bid and allowed the fates to decide whether Lot 21 came home with me later that day – which they did.

My first read-through of the letters was greedy as I skimmed the contents, omitting words that weren't immediately legible. I took in the essence of each one, but was no wiser by the finish as to the writers' identity or the stories they would weave for me in time. This initial hunger always passed and I spread the letters out in date order and began again with a magnifying glass, a notebook and a steadier heart. This was when each letter would unfold the past for me – sometimes using means that would have astonished the correspondents who began to draw breath and take shape with every sentence I transcribed.

> Monday 9th June 1856, Haddenham, Thame, Oxon.
>
> *My dear Miss Earle, I have no hesitation in trusting to your benevolence to excuse the trouble I am about to give you. You will be pleased to hear that Mrs Dawes arrived here in safety and in tolerable health, considering all things, at about ¼ past 2 on Thursday. - & the live stock she brought with her, including two maids & a black curly haired fellow, were also in tolerable plight: - but, alas! My poor Tippoo was wanting...*

Within a very short space of time W R Dawes is no longer a stranger to me and I know him to be William Rutter Dawes, a renowned astronomer who counted Sir John Herschel and William Lassell amongst his friends. William was born at Christ's Hospital, London on Tuesday 19th March 1799 and named William for his father and Rutter after his mother's maiden name – Judith Rutter.

The image I have formed is that of an elderly man, yet William was aged 57 when he wrote this letter in a spidery but legible hand. I soon become accustomed to the strokes of his pen and the peculiarities of letter writing in that period. It is akin to breaking a code but there is a continuity to his writing so that after a while I feel my way through the words and no longer find it strange that the first letter 's' of a double 's' sweeps up and then down and resembles a letter 'f'.

It might surprise teenagers today to see the abbreviations common in the writing of the 19th century and used to save space on the page just as text messaging saves time now. An ampersand usually replaced 'and'; longer words were often condensed by missing out some characters and superscripting the last two so that a letter might be signed, 'yours affec^{ly}'. Tunbridge Wells became 'TW' and words underlined for emphasis and importance just as a text message or email can now be 'shouted' by the use of capital letters. I can visualise William using textspeak so that *...with best wishes for your health & happiness, I remain, my dear Miss Earle, your faithful, friend...* would become B4N – bye for now.

Letter writers of the 19th century might have embraced the economy of textspeak but would perhaps have been reluctant to relinquish all their extravagant prose and polite phrases such as:

> *Pray do not hesitate to comply with my sincere request that you write fully to me at any time you imagine my advice may be of service to you. I need not say that I shall always esteem it a pleasure and a privilege to be in any way instrumental to your health and comfort.*

Such language would be considered 'OTT' now and ridiculed, but I find it comforting and would be happy to have someone poised to offer advice and attend to my well-being.

My impression is that William was sincere and also capable of resolving any problems – that he was wise and dependable. My enjoyment of his use of language is such that I am concerned that I will adopt it myself – indeed, I fear that I have already so embraced such prose that the lengthy emails I invariably compose, whilst deeply regretting the demise of letter writing, will become lengthier still with the use of eloquent phrases borrowed from William.

The clack and rattle of a keyboard is no substitute for the tactile pleasure of a virginal sheet of notepaper and a smooth flowing pen. I do not wish to be without the usefulness of a computer or the resources available through the internet but I feel it would be a tragedy if the familiarity of letter writing were to disappear. There is no delete key available when writing a letter by hand and care must be taken before the words are penned. Of course, words can be similarly weighed when typing at a keyboard but mistakes can easily be corrected rather than having to begin again.

Paper was not always simply paper and even now it is often measured and described in language that reaches back to when William wrote to Miss Earle. In an office supplies catalogue it is still possible to see paper described as vellum, parchment, laid and woven. Sadly, paper sizes have been reduced to a series of letters and numbers but William would have had the option of choosing writing paper that ranged from the smallest, Pott, to the largest, Double Elephant.

Foolscap was named for the fool's head and cap watermark once used on 15th century paper and is a paper size still in use, particularly in the legal profession. English watermarks indicated the size of paper so that if the watermark was intact and showed, for example, a *fleur-de-lis*, then the original size of the paper was Copy, and if, when you held the paper up to the light, a bugle appeared, then it was Post – no matter how small a fragment of either remained.

Fortunately, William chose a more manageable size for his letters, purchased ready folded as was usual, and I am beginning to 'see' the shadowy outline of this man as he draws fresh notepaper towards him. I feel as if I have been introduced to someone and am trying to assemble their character from overheard fragments of conversation. William was surely a kind man, caring enough to worry over the welfare of a missing pet and so familiar with Tippoo's day to day life that he could offer Miss Earle the following suggestions:

> *I have some fear that he may have concealed himself somewhere about the house, perhaps under the floor of the kitchen or study, where he used frequently to run when frightened: - or in one of the ash holes or flues of the coppers in the scullery. In this case, if the house is closed, the poor fellow may be starved. We should therefore greatly be obliged if you could ascertain whether he has been anywhere about, or if he is in the house or premises.*

Tippoo disappeared at the time of Mrs Dawes' departure from the house in Tunbridge Wells where the iron rich spa water was thought to be a remedy for many ailments – including the unpleasantly named 'moist brain'. The water is produced from a Chalybeate spring which, if at all similar to the tepid water served in the Pump Room at Bath, would have all the flavour of rusty nails. William was plagued with ill health for much of his life – with asthma and severe headaches – both of which were sure to be included in the list of illnesses curable by drinking the spa water.

Any physical features that I have imagined for William are put to the test when I find an image of him. The photograph depicts a William who looks directly at the camera, and at me, with dark, intelligent eyes. His spectacles are wire framed; his dark hair shows little grey and is receding but swept forward at the temples; his mouth reveals amiability in the upward curve at each corner in a way that also suggests a temperament more inclined towards good humour than ill temper. This was a time when men wore side-whiskers and William's appear soft and grey where they curl over a high collar.

I am certain that I am right to attribute William with a dependable character and a sensitive nature and I wish I could have one conversation with him. What would we speak about, William and me? Astronomy would be an obvious topic and although my contribution would be scant, William was known as Eagle-eyes Dawes for his observational skill at the telescope and could tell me about the many discoveries he made concerning double stars, or the crepe rings of Saturn.

Now I can 'see' my kindly, yet not so old, gentleman I need to know more and so return to the beginning; to William's beginning, as the son of a famous father.

Flash Fiction: Runner-up
Suzan Lindsay Randle

Picking up the Pieces

Sometimes Claude envied the street sweepers who worked for the council. They mostly had to collect discarded sweet wrappers and cigarette ends. Being an Emotional Environment Cleaning Specialist sounded quite grand but sweeping up bits of broken promises and shattered dreams took its toll. And there were some things he would never get used to, he thought, delicately picking up yet another piece of someone's heart and dropping it into his cart.

Short Story: Runner-up
Paul Brownsey

Human Relationships Under Capitalism

' – *BEWARE OF ADDERS,*' cries Simon, interrupting himself in mid-rant. 'Did you see that notice? Stop the car!' he insists in an irritated voice, as though he'd already said it once and been ignored. He's already out of the car as Barratt eases it onto grass and halts.

***

Driving south down the single-track Glen Gairn road had been a nervous negotiation of blind summits and concealed twists; passing places needed assiduous notice in case oncoming traffic, visible only at the last moment, threatened a head-on crash. But you also grew aware that the road was running high and the landscape had opened up like the heart can do. The smooth terrain descended westward in sunshine to motionless miniature distances, then rose to new heights, new enigmas, though there had been safe insulation in a news programme on the car radio and Simon's equable commentary on it.

'Market forces,' went an interviewed voice, 'can't any longer be left in control of our social and economic landscape. The credit crunch made *everyone* realise that.'

'Not me,' Simon replies cheerfully, in keeping with the fact that his red hair retains the sharp red of a young boy's instead of having sobered into the dirty brown appropriate to middle age. He still has the leanness of body, too, but also the freckles. He has accumulated 522 friends on Facebook.

'When this country,' says the voice with unpractised sincerity, 'decided that each person going all-out for his own private profit was the best way to advance the common good, the country bought an old wives' tale with no more credibility than the idea that you can't get pregnant the first time.'

'Nice,' says Simon in unfeigned admiration of the wit of the comparison, but he continues immediately: 'So it's to be tax rates at 95% again, state control of every fucking thing, and we've all got to get teary about the so-called needy –' He's jolted by a sudden swerve for which there's no obvious reason. ' – Careful! – the fucking so-called needy who only need to get up off their arses and *do* something instead of taking the easy option of dependency culture. And the *government* running industry, for God's sake. Destroying us. Squeezing us out.'

'The anaconda of the state,' says Barratt loyally, and he has every reason to mean it because their business – signing up and hiring out nurses – had gone down the pan after the National Health Service set up its own nurse banks and also started getting picky about the qualifications of agency nurses, even though most of them had been trained by the NHS in the first place.

The rounded snout of a ridge appears across the valley, an imagined hillside in a sixteenth-century painting, tiny trees cresting it as though marching to something good, perhaps to a bower where gods and men dwell in perfect harmony.

'The anaconda of the state.' Barratt said it not only loyally but gratefully, too, since Simon didn't mention his guilt. Barratt knows he'd not been a good businessman, too timid or something, too little drive or self-esteem. 'It's just...' he'd say, petering out, and, 'But what's the use?' Simon, uncomprehending, had demonstrated time and again how a nursing agency was to everyone's advantage, the NHS able to call on extra nurses precisely when it needed them, the nurses – many of them single mums – welcoming the flexibility of not being shackled by fixed hours and a permanent contract of employment, and themselves rightly rewarded by 33% commission for their initiative. He'd rebuked Barratt: 'Your parents wouldn't have had any sentimentality about it. They bought their council house as soon as Mrs Thatcher freed them to and sold it on at a good profit.'

'And fucking unions,' Simon continues as Barratt slows for a lamb that seems not to know which side of the road its mother is on and runs from side to side bleating, 'holding the country to ransom with their so-called demands, no heat or light in the depths of winter because the miners or electricity workers or some other load of shits are holding the country to ransom, exploiting people's basic needs to get more money... I *remember* those nights in the 70s without electricity, Barry.' He says the last bit as though he'd never mentioned it in the nineteen years they were together. 'Doing my homework by candlelight. The exercise-book caught fire.'

'Demands,' says Barratt.

'What?'

'They were demands, not so-called demands.' But this dig is ingratitude after Simon hasn't for a long while now alluded to the blameworthy things Barratt did like telling hospitals that Nursing Help Service (Scotland) wouldn't claim the whopping introduction fees that its terms and conditions allowed it to charge when hospitals gave permanent jobs to people who'd first been supplied on an agency basis. Barratt says, 'Fucking pillocks.' He nods towards a red Skoda on their left. In his heavy sagging face the lips remain cherubic, unfit for swear-words. 'Parking in a passing place. They could cause a fucking accident.'

Two women in thick old-fashioned blue shorts made purely for use and not for style, so their white legs look stringy and unfeminine, are ascending the hillside above the Skoda. They hold tall staves, not modern walking poles.

'It wasn't a parking place. It was off the road,' Simon retaliates for that little dig about *so-called*, which obviously came from lingering resentment because Simon, as he had a perfect right to, had ended the relationship after the business failed. When Simon could feel they were a pair of buccaneers in alliance, engaged in the war of all against all for the world's booty, everything was fine between them. It had been flattering, a testimony to Simon's own power, to think of Barratt as an independent operator who'd hooked up with him just because it was profitable to Barratt to do so. The charge between them was even enhanced, at least on Simon's side, by awareness that they could have been business enemies.

But when financial disaster came and they learned that the Edinburgh house in Easter Belmont Road for which they'd triumphantly paid a million needed to be sold to pay debts, Barratt had felt like a liability, too. 'We've still got each other,' Barratt said, but Simon, wriggling out of his arms, had to explain that they were no longer partners in any meaning of the word.

He'd said, 'You invested too much in the relationship, Barry. You've got to cut your losses and move on. You're too dependent, Barry. Needy.'

As Barratt noses the Volvo over the steep old hump-backed bridge over the Gairn at the heart of the glen, immensely picturesque though not built to be picturesque, Simon can still admire his own wit when, having begun sleeping with a nurse who wore nothing under his scrubs, he'd described it as 'salvaging one of the firm's assets'. He'd been pleased that Barratt fell into the spirit of the thing, telling people even in Simon's presence, 'He's trading me in for a younger model,' and once Simon replied, with a thrilling realism which created a sort of intimacy of its own, 'You'd have done the same except that a pot belly is not a commodity for which there's much market demand.' And Barratt had even continued the joke, replying, as he slapped his belly, 'Too much of a competitive edge.' But the luxury country-house hotel wouldn't let them cancel even though circumstances had changed, and the small print outrageously allowed the thieving bastards, who had taken credit card details along with the booking, to charge the full cost even if they didn't turn up, so Simon had decreed going ahead with the holiday anyway. 'Just as friends,' he'd warned.

Now a different radio voice is responding to the earnest one to ensure balance, a statesman's public voice tuned to public truth, making private thoughts feel impertinent and helpless.

'The *right* course of action has to be taken. That is essential to our country's future. What Victoria would like is to turn the clock back to socialism, but the hard-earned experience of the last half-century is that socialism is a failed experiment. Eastern Europe was our laboratory. We *know*, know on the basis of irrefutable evidence, what happens when bureaucrats interfere in the natural processes of wealth creation, in the free market. Competition, hard but fair competition, forces up quality and forces down prices, and stifling it is an attack on prosperity and freedom *for all*.'

'Not to mention,' says Simon comfortably, 'an attack on my, our, everyone's right to do what they want with their *own* money instead of having it *stolen* by the state and handed out to people for whom living on benefits is a lifestyle choice, the feckless and the scroungers and the idiot thirteen-year-old girls who can't wait to be 'single mums' like their mothers and grandmothers. The so-called needy. *So-called* used correctly there. – *BEWARE OF ADDERS*. Did you see that notice? Stop the car!' He's already out of the car as Barratt eases it onto grass and halts.

***

In the silence a lark sings and they remark almost in chorus, 'The Lark Ascending', this being the name of a piece of music that, they have read, accumulated most votes in a poll to decide the nation's most in-demand piece of classical music

‘*BEWARE OF ADDERS*. That’s amazing,’ says Simon, touching the anonymous words, crude as a blackmailing letter, hand-painted on a board nailed to a post. ‘Why would someone put up a notice like that?’ He looks to Barratt as though for answer, an entirely unrehearsed survival of their nineteen-year relationship. But Simon provides the authoritative answer himself. ‘It’s an attempt by some sheep-shagging farmer to scare people off his land. He doesn’t like it that we’ve got the right to roam now and this is him trying to deny us our rights.’

The notice stands sentinel before a gully and naturally makes one think of the path up through it as *snaking* upwards through the bracken and heather and blaeberry bushes, all motionless in the sun, no waves in them to mark the passage of slithering serpents. The lark sings on.

‘Or,’ says Barratt, and it’s more like joining in a practised duet than offering a dissenting opinion, ‘maybe it’s because of people parking in the passing places. To make them terrified to stop anywhere.’

‘No, I’ve got it,’ cries Simon delightedly, in a voice acknowledging that this is a joint discovery after a joint enquiry, ‘it’s just nastiness, plain and simple. Someone just taking pleasure in frightening people. Malice. Well, he’s not frightening *me*,’ and in his trainers (Diesel Black Gold Positive Military, £120) he begins a sort of hop-step dance in and among the clumps of heather and bracken and blaeberry bushes. ‘No fucking adders here.’

Barratt watches him as though he’s to give him theatrical notes on his performance. He says, ‘But aren’t they timid? Won’t all that clumping about just drive them away anyway?’

Without ceasing his hop-step Simon tugs off trainers and socks.

‘Bare feet... That’ll hurt.’

‘Not a bit! No fucking adders here!’

And then he peels off his t-shirt (Westwood Gold Graphic, £97) and like one sort of stripper twirls it over his head and flings it aside. He dances on, then hurls himself onto the heather and commences rolling about, this way and that, throwing himself up and down and over and around, sending into the air sun-warmed puffs of earthy or vegetable particles. ‘No fucking adders here! – Aaauuh!’ The yell is triggered, not by a snake, but by a grouse suddenly shooting up with its accelerating cry like a guttural motor, and in reply, Simon, on his feet again, peels off the combat trousers (Maharishi £150) and underpants (Dolce and Gabbana £26.72) and his Red Indian dance is now entirely naked and he's whooping, 'No fucking adders here!' as he slowly circles back towards Barratt.

There's a slablike outcrop of rock, scaly with grey-black lichen, and in sudden exhaustion Simon sits down, then leaps up again, not because he's lowered his arse onto a serpent basking in the sun, as they are said to like to do, but because the rocky sharpnesses hurt his buttocks. Barratt has been moving about in the heather and bracken, gathering up the abandoned garments, stamping his feet to drive away adders before cautiously and quickly reaching for each item. He hands the t-shirt to Simon, who throws it under himself and sits again. Awkward with the remaining clothes, Barratt tries to sit on the slab, too, but the angle and shape make this difficult and he can sit only back to back with Simon.

The lark is singing again, or perhaps it always was, or perhaps it's a different one; no, there are two, three, and there's a faint deep background hum as though stillness is being made audible by sunshine. Barratt stares towards a clump of pink-purple blossoms with the artificial brightness and homogeneity of something dipped in industrial dye: bell heather among the common heather. A kind of peace settles, the churning up of the vegetation by Simon's dance might never have happened, and the land in its heights and distances is benign. 'The power of nature,' murmurs Barratt, incurious about the camouflage-like patchwork of different greens and browns on the hills that results from annual burnings dictated by grouse-rearing for the shooting industry. As for the ruined cottage just discernible in a sheltering dip of the land, easier testimony that this landscape has been shaped by generations of people making a living – well, it's a *ruined* cottage, merely picturesque; nature is reclaiming dominion.

And as they sit silently, back to back, sweaty Simon recovering his breath, feels smarting and throbbing up through his naked body what he was oblivious to during his dance, namely, all the multifarious pains from scratches and scrapes and sharp poking digs. Feeling, too, the hard line of Barratt's belt (Mac's Handystore, £3.99) against his back, he experiences an erection founded on awareness of Barratt, the first since the business failed, despite the past week of sharing a bedroom with him. As though Barratt senses this, he reaches behind him and awkwardly pats one of Simon's self-marketing enterprises, a very incomplete six-pack.

'You're too needy.' Unhand me, sir.

'Too right.' But the hand stays put; stays put in supplication.

Or *is* it supplication?

Yes, Barratt's emotional dependency is no advantage, a fetter, something to shrink from. Yet it could also be said that he has been playing a long game to repossess the asset he wants, namely, himself, Simon, enduring all sorts of, well, cruelties until the moment is ripe for the merger. Even his acquiescence there in his own neediness – 'Too right' – was a clever move in the struggle by a something that's independent, scheming, self-moving, relentless. In the right light – in this unclouded sunlight, for instance, that bakes all fret and pretension out of the landscape – Barratt has something that looks alluringly like power.

On their awkward rock Simon swivels on his tee-shirt and takes Barratt, still clutching Simon's clothes to him, in his arms as best he can and kisses him passionately.

The trainers drop. Barratt pulls away. 'No, look...' He's bending to right the trainers, placing them neatly side by side. There's the sweet warm crushed smell of bracken. 'I don't want it to be only, like, here and now. Because, like, you suddenly fancy open-air sex.'

Simon admires this move. He's read somewhere that Richard Branson, just when people think they've got a contract sewn up with him, suddenly reopens a point they thought was settled and gets new concessions out of them, which is perfectly natural, evolution teaching us that people are always out to get advantage for themselves and put one over on competitors: the struggle for existence, the selfish gene, etc. Counting the times he's met Richard Branson, he says, 'Okay,' before he realises he was going to say it.

'And Desmond?' he ventures: 'The scrubber in scrubs?'

'I'll let him go.'

But Simon's not so weak he couldn't have held out for a better deal from a clingy person who always gave more in the relationship than he did; a person who's blameworthy, too. Simon shakes his head, sighs, looks at Barratt tolerantly. 'Never really lived up to the significance of your name, did you?'

This alludes to the fact that, parents having the right to call children anything they want to, the children being *theirs*, he was named after his parents' aspiration to own a Barratt home, of which there had seemed no hope in their council house back in the 1960s when his mother had been an assiduous visitor of show homes.

‘Named after a symbol of aspiration, and you couldn’t hack it. Wouldn’t push hard enough, not focused. Our business was perfectly legitimate, Barry. Perfectly legal. There was a market opportunity and we took it.’

‘All I can say is, I’m sorry,’ says Barratt ruthlessly.

Soon Barratt’s clothes are off, too, and they are making love on their rock, but it’s too hard and uncomfortable, and they slide down into the heather. There are in Simon the trembling beginnings of a new thought about *BEWARE OF ADDERS* but it is drowned by the distant first intimations of orgasm, and they are like two bees nuzzling the common heather, oblivious to landscape vistas that open up like the heart, but they are themselves observed, for two female hikers in blue shorts look down from above, their faces not shocked or amused or prurient but merely tender.

Creative Non-fiction Essay: Runner-up

Moy McCrory

Joan of Arc, Ringo Starr & Me

Strange thing was, back then, if people heard you came from Liverpool they always asked if you knew the Beatles. Like Americans who, on hearing an English accent, want to know when you last saw the Queen, Beatlemania operated the same way. Back then if people heard a Liverpool accent, that was it, they'd be at you for details. Like you'd known them when they were playing out in the street, when they were lads hanging round corners or walking back from the chippy. Of course, it didn't work like that and even those who had asked knew it in the first place and used to laugh at their own expectations.

No, I'd tell people, grinning. And I don't know The Queen either.

But I always felt embarrassed because I had in fact grown up across the way from Ringo. And I had never once seen him.

He was always the odd Beatle anyway, the least fancied and the least fabulous of the four. A drummer; and you know what they say about drummers. Squealing girls think they are the consolation prizes for the groupies who didn't cop-off with the vocalist.

It was just before full blown Beatlemania in those early days when I was still too young to understand what everyone wanted with the boys but, already in the city, news was spreading.

My mate's much older brother was a Cavern habitué. He started wearing his hair differently that summer and let us have his Country & Western collection, which we played on a Dansette, stacking the discs and watching them crash as the robot arm clicked them to drop. We were as fascinated by the technology as the music, but all the while the airwaves were playing new sounds. That was the summer we learnt to dance the twist. Everybody was twisting *again,* as if we had forgotten it the first time round and Chubby Checker went on a world tour and went home two stones lighter after sweating it out on Sunday nights at the London Palladium. And there they were. These four lads without short back and sides, belting out rock and roll.

Adults were taking it seriously, this heavy driven beat you couldn't avoid. It seeped in everywhere; on radios and transistors in the park, public places were full of this music, it was a different sound, one which made matrons light on their feet and caused little kids to walk up the road to church singing. One friend's mother cut the wires at home as parents began to worry what might happen to us if we became swept up in this new craze. Already people were twisting like maniacs at family weddings, aunties and uncles danced like they were stubbing out cigarettes, little kids twisted at birthday parties after musical chairs and pass the parcel – we all twisted like loons. We wore twist dresses with dropped waists which made them long in the body and fanned out at the skirt. I had a turquoise twist dress made from a pair of old curtains and my aunt gave my mother some broken jewellery that she fashioned into a chain for round my hips. I loved that dress with its glittering belt and wore it for ever until my brother didn't screw the cap back on the ketchup and I picked up the bottle to shake it and my beautiful frock was ruined with stains which wouldn't wash out, but left it faded and shrunken like something I had already outgrown.

Most parents reckoned twisting was socially safe although the Liverpool Echo carried stories of people hospitalised with slipped discs, but this new beat was harder and the audience was different. Adults consoled themselves that it would burn out soon, all be over by the time we were teenagers, terrified by these strange new beings who owned the streets, striding down pavements in jeans. Corner boys my father dubbed them. Eeejits made good. 'And what will happen to them once this is all over?' people muttered. No good will come of it.

Those days young men took up apprenticeships, got work in shipyards or on the docks, maybe got a profession although no one we knew had a clue how you went about that. You put your name down for the post office or a soft job in the Liver Buildings or maybe the bank because that was decent. But the likes of these fellers, on the wireless now, they'll have nothing at all, they said. Nothing at all but memories of playing music in a cave. What sort of training is that?

'Any auld eejit can bang a bleddy drum,' my father said once, having watched Look North about the rise of the Mersey beat. But by that time the four had beat it, out of Liverpool and fast to London.

But I have this memory of a dark sleek car turning up one night and the neighbours coming out to watch because cars were enough of a novelty in this part of the city. My mother, quick off the mark as usual, thought someone had died, for this had to be a hearse which was the only large car she had ever seen. The car waited in

High Park Street as the narrow turning behind the pub where it was calling was not open to traffic. Beige concrete bollards the texture of solidified porridge stood in the way, not exactly sentinels but something local and guarded. Something important was taking place in that small tight knot of streets where we, as Catholics, never ventured.

I grew up in a corner house in a zone that had been earmarked for redevelopment with flattened bomb sites for playgrounds. I went to the local Catholic school and the solitary Beatle who lived in our working class area of Toxteth went to school at Saint Silas, who was an obscure but decidedly Protestant figure. It wasn't just my age which meant I never once saw Ringo when he was still a teenager living there. My friend's older brother, a few years younger than Ringo, would never have rubbed shoulders with him at school either. There was a cultural divide which felt as if we lived in different countries sometimes, even in the same narrow streets as we passed neighbours on their way to separate churches.

Our house was on the corner of a narrow group of streets known as the Welsh streets, not because of the inhabitants but on account of the builders who worked on the sites. So it was named Gwydir Street – or Green Street. High Park Street ran down the rows of terraces and bisected us, often into allegiances. Across the main street was the pub where my parents wouldn't set foot, in case the neighbours saw them. It was, they claimed, a rough awful place full of drunks and no goods; The Empress of Russia. I thought then that the pub's image was of Queen Victoria because any old and treble-chinned woman looked to me like the famous statue down town by the bus station, standing erect with her mace. So we kept ourselves apart. Those few small streets across the way where Ringo had grown up were as foreign to me as that exotic saying 'On the Continent' which I only heard on the TV, usually from a man in a suit reading the news. We seemed to develop our own pastimes; while they roundly condemned drink, all the adults I knew considered sweet eating serious business. Most of them wore false teeth. Responsible fathers saved in order to give their daughters a good set in time for their wedding. A sign of maturity, women embarked on married life with false ivory smiles, the same hard smiles which would be set in their mouths for the last time by the corpse dresser. Teeth were a status symbol for, along with burial policies, the tooth club was the only form of saving we had. On Thursdays the Club-Man called. He wore a long Macintosh and wrote everything down in spectacular copperplate. We carried our burial price, dreading the pauper's funeral.

'No family of mine is going to make a show of themselves after they're dead,' my mother said and presented us with the deeds to our plots as we reached the age of ten by way of a birthday present. There weren't many other distractions. My father went to the theatre only once. It was a play the Catholic Pictorial recommended about the Irish arriving in Liverpool. That was the first time I heard that we (meaning my parents, and preceding generations) had been a problem for the local populace. My father thought it would be an education for us, so we went along to sit in the dark. Throughout the play he ate boiled sweets, unwrapping cellophane and crunching with his false teeth. My mother was an exceptional woman because she had all her own and preferred savouries. As he ate his way through the first act, heads turned in our direction. People shushed and glared at me and my brother.

Snobs, my father remarked in the interval, Bloody English.

Throughout the performance every time an actor swore on stage my father would stare round wildly and tut. God knows, there might have been someone there who knew him. It still felt like a small place then where people knew you and would be quick to name a misdeed as a good one, yet seeing that sleek car that night and the neighbours talking out on the streets as they stood to watch the local boy being picked up by his manager, we were oblivious of what was happening. Ringo's spurt of fame mattered little to us. Our area was already full of celebrities. There was Joan of Arc who had been brought home once in a police car after she had been found wandering in the bus terminal asking which one went to France. We had even had Jesus living among us when I was very small, though not for long because his family had him sectioned. And there was Crazy Phyllis whose baby, they told me, had died so she had tried to take another from outside the Co-op. She would walk down the middle of the main road – there were few cars then and the buses were not routed to come that way but skirted our district by the top and bottom roads, from Park Road and the Boulevard as if someone had tipped them off that motors needed to avoid us. Twenty years later in the Toxteth riots that area became a transport no-go zone again, only that time it was with burning car tyres and not a taxi prepared to go there.

And then there was the shouting man who stood on corners and spoke in tongues, they reckoned. Later the milkman became a celebrity of sorts, but only after he killed himself. The neighbours couldn't understand it, they said he was only a boy really. It was his mother who found him and being widowed had had to cut him down herself. The neighbours said things like 'Who'd have thought it? He was always whistling.'

With so much celebrity I think no one noticed Ringo Starr. He must have just grown up quietly in that street behind the Empress, where no one we knew would go for a drink because behind that pub were unfamiliar streets and we didn't go that way unless it was raining and we needed a short cut.

Some years later after the Beatles had long left the city we would find a gaggle of strangely dressed girls with odd sounding accents waiting outside the house, or photographing the front door. Once I watched transfixed as a girl performed a strange ritual. She slowly touched the four corners of the door then crossed her arms then re-crossed the door the other way round, from right to left, then knelt on the step and bowed her head. Like those who struggle out to Juliet's balcony in Verona, she had come to seek a blessing from a tangible site of pilgrimage, but the occasion for it was long gone. Ringo's family had moved out, possibly exhausted by pilgrims such as this though most probably at their son's insistence that he get them a bigger place.

Odd the things you remember – a boy my own age walked past and dropped a kitten at our feet. He told us it had been sick and his ma had told him to dump it. We stood frozen, staring at this small mewling thing and suddenly the pilgrim girl was upon us as the lad walked off.

'You be cruel to that cat and I'll be cruel to you!' she yelled in what I can now describe as an American accent. We were rooted to the pavement, condemned and found guilty. My friend tried to explain, but this girl was adamant as she stood there glowing with zeal, a strange saint, patron of abandoned kittens, so we walked off and left the animal to its certain death. That was our neighbourhood. Touch all the doors you like, nothing would make it different.

The girl stands out. She was as exotic as the pineapple I had been taken to see the previous Saturday. It had turned up in the grocer's like an alien life-form. My father had seen it on his way back from work on Friday.

Comb your hair and wash your face, he told me.

By the time we arrived a queue had gathered outside the shop and was filing past the window with as much reverence as communists once viewed Lenin. The pineapple sat there all day. No one dared ask how much it was. No one had a clue how to eat it. It was bought at last by the priest's housekeeper who wheeled it to the presbytery in her shopper followed by a straggle of children in procession. For some years after in our district pineapple was still referred to as holy fruit. No one knew what we were talking about.

So the first thing most of us knew about Ringo was this long black car parked outside the turn off that would later house a shrine before the council pulled the streets down for clearance. This was Brian Epstein whose father owned the music shop down town, and he had just become the manager of a group Ringo played in. They had signed a contract so it must have been legal. Brian Epstein's photo was in the Liverpool Echo because his group was going to make a record and he was looking to sign up other acts.

My mate's older brother stood in front of the kitchen mirror combing his hair forward into a fringe. Brylcreem were going bankrupt. He said they were dead good the lot Ringo was with, but there were others who were crap and Brian Epstein was signing them too.

By the time Brian's group appeared on our small TV screen in black and white, they felt as distant and remote as the pictures which would later come from the moon, which I watched on holiday in the Isle of Man and my mother said what terrible weather it was to be going all that way in and why hadn't they at least waited till it stopped bucketing down, hadn't those men enough to contend with steering a bloody rocket?

People always asked then, when they heard you came from Liverpool, if you knew the Beatles. But by the time I was old enough to blag my still underage way into the Cavern, they had disbanded. I was living in London when John Lennon was shot in New York. They were never part of what I knew; the crazy people shouting from windows, the desperate women with eyes like flint, the rolling drunks when the pubs let out those who kept us awake with their swearing and carousing. And the fathers who had told their sons to get proper jobs and not end up like soft-lad over the road. 'There's no future in it', they said, and 'What sort of a job is that banging a drum? Couldn't any fool do that?'

When the newsagent committed suicide they knew it was no accident. Frogmen found him washed up on the Wirral, the pockets of his heavy duty mac weighed down with stones. He'd stepped off the landing stage after the last ferry and let himself sink down into the Mersey. Grainy CCTV played back the moment at the inquest. None of my mother's neighbours could understand why. But he was always telling jokes, they said. If he'd just stuck with papers he'd still be here they told each other. But he'd branched out into groceries.

My mother worried about the eggs and all that milk going sour, not to mention the loaves of bread. 'It's dreadful,' she said, 'when there's people starving on the telly.' And he'd taken the keys to the lock-up with him. But as for the newspapers, sure what good was yesterday's news to anyone now?

When Brian Epstein killed himself they said 'Didn't I tell you?' and 'That's where it gets you.'

People stopped asking if you knew the Beatles as time wore on. A Liverpool accent does not court instant approval any more, if it ever really did. There are still those who will tell you that Liverpool was a great place to be back then. Oddly enough, I don't remember anyone saying so at the time.

Flash Fiction: Runner-up
Michael Palmer

The Birds and the Light in Pedro Carbo

In the day I met my brother's friends and at night I confronted the birds. In the day the sunlight dripped onto our skins and at night the darkness spilled into our ears and eyes. In the day my brother spoke Spanish and I tried to absorb it; at night we both spoke English, and sometimes he would forget how to pronounce words like 'terminal'. In the day I ordered coffee or milk or orange soda and at night I mixed rum with my coke and I did it on the sly because my brother was strongly offended by alcohol. In the day we could talk with Alberto about the birds, of which he was very proud. Besides managing the hotel, Alberto was into cockfighting. He was a mad geneticist of sorts and experimentally bred different birds together, hoping to come up with breeds that would be good fighters. At night Alberto was asleep and the birds were there without any explanation. In the day, Alberto told us that of all the birds he was most impressed by the eagle chickens, which according to him are what they sound like: the result of an eagle bred with a chicken. Whatever they were, they were dark monstrosities with yellow eyes and they lingered on bushes that were very low to the ground. They never flew, they never walked around, they just sat on those bushes and made a horrible sound, like a tired, old cat falling down the stairs. At night those birds were harder to identify, but you knew they were in the bushes somewhere. In the day we paid fifty cents to ride in the back of a pickup truck out to some farms. My brother knew some people there. At night we rode in the back of the same truck but didn't talk the whole way. In the day we had to decide if we wanted to head back early so we could get to the hotel before Alberto locked the front door and went to bed; at night we had to regret not getting there earlier and having to go around back and walk through the valley of birds. At night, the bright yellow eyes of the eagle chickens floated in the darkness like crocodile eyes just above the water.

1st Chapter of a Creative Non-fiction Book: Runner-up
Penny Wolfson

Ephemera: A Memoir in Objects

In January of 2004, my mother died after a brief illness. We had not expected her death, though she was 82; just a week before she had been very alive, on her own in a walk-up apartment, tending to her grandchildren, planning birthday parties for friends, using her skills as a reading specialist to teach adult literacy classes at a local community college.

One evening she fainted and fell in her apartment. Her doctor, who lived in her building and was immediately on the scene, had her taken to the ER, where she was found to have a bleeding ulcer. (I remember helping her sit up on a gurney and sensing how suddenly weightless she'd become; I remember, too, the pinkish young skin I saw on her midriff as the sheet shifted, and how odd and intimate that seemed; I remember that all she wanted was a pillow, and that there were none to be found.) She should have recovered, and after receiving several pints of blood she did rally; for a day or two she seemed like her old self, enjoying the coffee *hopjes* candies I had brought for her and the photos of the new litter of kittens in my house. But after a week and a day in the hospital, she was struck down, abruptly, by a pulmonary embolism, and just like that, poof, she was gone.

It was a terrible shock for us – it was hard not to love my mother, unthinkable to contemplate a future without her – but for her I think less so. She had, it seemed to me, made up her mind in the months since her 80th birthday to prepare for her death by giving away many of her things to us. (She also during that period wrote an 'Ethical Will' which was an articulation of the credos by which she lived.) So during those two years I remember her driving from Long Island up to Westchester with my also-elderly aunt and schlepping up the front steps, swathed in sheets of bubble wrap, the enormous Delft platter she and my father had received for a wedding gift from their employers, a Dutch family called the deSwaans, and which always sat, pretty much unnoticed, on a living room shelf; and another time bringing, in several patched-together cartons, the blue-and-gold etched-glass vases and matching covered jar that she told me my father had brought back from Czechoslovakia years before. These had perhaps been hidden in the 'breakfront' in the dining room or stuck on the mantel during my childhood; I don't remember.

I think also she brought me during that period the deep-blue and silver-tipped Wedgwood sugar and creamer set we never used, and the pounded silver *embraceros,* the enormous bracelets from Peru I'd never seen her wear but had sat in her jewellery box for decades.

I know we didn't really appreciate these, she seemed to be saying now, wordlessly pushing the boxes across the dining room table in my direction, but I know you will.

I had not really thought of my mother as a keeper or preserver of objects, not objects of any real value or beauty, anyway. It's true she had kept all of our birthday cards, classified in a rough order, in several ungainly, slipshod and sometimes downright ugly notebooks, binders and albums, as well as other ephemera that obviously held meaning for her: programmes from Hebrew school graduations, the leatherette case from the *Government in Action* conference I attended in Washington my senior year of high school, the menus as well as the anesthesiologist's bills from her maternity stays in the hospital when each of us four girls was born – in other words, mostly junk that should have been tossed years before. Having come from nothing herself – a shtetl girl whose father ran a dry goods store on Mermaid Avenue in Coney Island – she tended to scoff at *things*, whether they were art objects or fur coats – and to focus on other people's needs. Hers was the mindset of the immigrant, the transient, the wandering Jew, the one who expects the rug to be literally pulled up under her feet, and so the rug was probably not worth having. Things could not be trusted.

In fact, the objects in my mother's *stories* were much more vivid to me than the objects that existed around us. These stories were delivered to me after Shabbos dinner on Friday nights with a slice of marble loaf and the weak, milkless tea we drank after a meat meal. My father and my sisters would have gone to bed already, but my mother and I would sit up late, talking, in the dining room with its scalloped doorways and yellowed wallpaper that featured a large repetitive pattern depicting scenes of Olde New York – horse and carriages, women in stiff bonnets and long dresses with frills – wallpaper to which I felt unaccountably, nostalgically attached, as though I had lived through those long-ago decades.

There are three stories I remember; she must have narrated them many times. The first was this: As a small child, my mother lived with her own mother and maternal grandparents in a village not far from Warsaw, called Nacielcz. There isn't much left of this family, these Blasskas – or for that matter, of the Jewish population of Nacielcz – but my understanding is my grandfather was a brewer. My mother's father, afraid he might be drafted into the newly formed Polish army, had fled to America in 1920, when his wife was newly pregnant with my mother, their second child. But that's just background; the story my mother told was about her episode of scarlet fever. They used the traditional remedy – cupping, *bankes,* my mother said, using the Yiddish term – and shaved off all her hair to reduce the fever. She said little about the cupping, leaving this to my imagination, but about losing her hair she spoke: even at four, she said, she had felt the nakedness of her bald head, the exposure, the defeminisation. But her own mother was not tuned in to such subtle emotion. Perhaps she was thinking of her own far-off husband or her problematic, effeminate son.

'Well, *you* know my mother,' she said, and I instantly thought of my elderly, difficult grandmother – the only grandparent I had ever known – who spent her life, it seemed to me, reading the *Daily Forward* in Yiddish by some dying light, asking me to thread a needle so she could mend our clothes, or incongruously, cooking us Ronzoni 'wagon wheels' and cold tomato sauce from the can for lunch.

'You know,' this grandmother would say, surveying me slowly with a birdlike eye, 'what you're wearing, darling; it clashes' – astonishing, because she knew so little English. Why was it she had learned the word 'clash'? And why did she know that I of all her grandchildren would be driven the most crazy by that criticism?

'Lieber Pesah, *she* knew,' my mother interrupts my imagining and stirs her tea. Lieber Pesah was her grandmother who, sensing the girl's grief, immediately came up with one of her own brightly coloured scarves to wrap around Tema's little head – her *keppele – to* love and encircle her. That I was named for this grandmother, that this grandmother died of 'a broken heart' when the rest of the family finally sailed for America, that one treated a child not just with love but with respect, that a child could possess untold depths of sadness and humiliation, that my mother was hereby handing down the invisible heirlooms of self, of her lived life – none of this was lost on me.

In the second story, her father began to figure. When my mother arrived in New York in 1926, in second-class, on the Aquitania – 'Sister ship of the Lusitania,' she always reminded me, as if I understood the grandeur implied – she had never met her father. Like many immigrants of that generation, he had come before his family, scouting out the territory, as it were, finding work, establishing himself. My mother arrived in America with her brother and her mother; a mournful looking five-year-old with short black curls encircled by a narrow ribbon, dark eyes, expressively peaked brows. In her passport picture she is wearing a wide collared dress and leaning her rather large head, posed, against a chair. She looks alarmed.

Her father, Yisroel Salzman, was in his mid-twenties, presumably a man with little experience of children. (He remains a potent mystery to me, a Torah scholar who liked the ladies, a man so vain he wore lipstick, a man who till his dying day – at 48, of a heart attack – still had all of his hair.)

'So I've never met him before. I come off the boat. And he's there, with a doll. A baby doll.'

She pauses, adds more hot water to her cup and squeezes out with a spoon her by-now anaemic teabag.

'I hated him on sight, and the doll, too.'

'Why?'

She shrugs in answer to my question. 'I don't know why. Maybe I just didn't know him. As simple as that. I was afraid. And I thought I was too grown up for a baby doll. So I threw the doll away.'

She muses on this for a moment, considering with some amusement and regret her ancient, childish decision. 'And later I was sorry, of course. Because I didn't ever get another one.'

Thus was set up a contrary relationship, which would last for the rest of her father's life.

The third story introduced her father as villain; it was the most disturbing of all. This was a tale calculated to bring all my mother's sense of injustice and simmering anger to the fore, to explain to me what was right and wrong in the world. Her cousin Chaim was studying for his bar mitzvah. Every afternoon he'd stop by the store on Mermaid Avenue to say hello. He'd give her candy, help her with schoolwork. A brilliant boy, she tells me. Then, tragedy: Chaim is struck down by appendicitis one night. My grandfather, who apparently owned a car – in the 1930s! – refused to take the kid to the hospital despite my mother's begging. Instead her uncle Morris took him in his milk truck, laying him on the rough wooden planks in the back. The boy did not survive; it's obvious my mother thinks her father brought about his death.

'They had already bought his bar mitzvah suit; that was the terrible thing,' she said, and I could as a child practically hear the hollow metallic sound of the hanger holding the suit, swinging back and forth in the boy's otherwise empty closet. How, too, that never-seen flowered scarf bloomed in my imagination, how clearly I could see the abandoned doll floating in New York Harbour! My mother, probably unbeknownst to her, was transmitting to me an understanding of the symbolic nature of *things*.

My father's melodramas were not in his stories; they didn't need to be, since the complex and occasionally tragic events of his youth – poverty, bankruptcy, death – were filled in willingly by his sisters; anyway we had a nearly daily showing of his *Sturm* and *Drang* in the form of his mercurial personality. In this day and age he would no doubt be considered bipolar, with his sudden rages and sudden tenderness; he often made my early life scary and miserable. But his stories were surprisingly fanciful, and I realize now they were part of a self-mythology that must have kept him emotionally afloat in his early years. The stories I remember best were in fact based in objects, in this case two pink porcelain mice sold to my parents as a salt and pepper shaker set in the gift shop of the Brooklyn Children's Museum. I doubt we ever used them in the kitchen; my memory is we played with them as toys. And my father seemed particularly taken with them: he gave them names – Horatio and Horace – and had them set sail around the world in a series of made-up trips he relayed in a bunch of bedtime stories, whose substance now escapes me. He was not generally that imaginative a fellow, nor that playful, and it surprises and pleases me now to remember that side of him.

I can't help thinking Horatio and Horace were stand-ins for himself, Henry, on his wonderful adventures around the world. I never really understood this about my father – that he'd always wanted to travel – until, 17 years after his death, I found among his things the only artefact left from his childhood: a notebook labelled OUR LEADER and filled with clippings about Lindbergh, who took his historic flight when my father was 13. My father was *meant* to travel.

We had been hoodwinked into believing that he had got into business by chance, that he was a scientist manqué, robbed of his chance of working in a chemistry laboratory by what really added up to a minor radiation accident. (He apparently sat on a container of polonium sometime in 1947 and had flu-like symptoms for some time. He was tested at MIT for many years afterward; no specific long-term effect was ever found.)

No, he loved business, and he loved the edgy risks of travel. Or maybe he was simply taking flight from the established routine of home life, the responsibilities he had taken on, in the form of family and mortgages and stability. He required romance.

The travel was for business; he always went alone, and it took him around the globe every year until the late 1970s. His first trip was to Lima, Peru, in 1949 for the Canadian Radium and Uranium Company; his last trip was to India, as it had been for the previous 20 years, when he worked for a Dutch firm called Deswaan, which imported jute from the East.

He travelled and he brought us things, often beautiful. Some stand out: wooden shoes, Droste chocolates, dolls from Greece and India and the Caribbean, a skirt from Carnaby Street in London – then the hippest address in the world – a *hapi* coat from Japan. Once he brought a walnut shell that when pried open revealed a miniature shrine. He brought back bolts of rich brocaded Indian cloth and an ivory tusk upon which a line of tiny carved elephants ascended. There were some little beans plugged up with a bit of ivory which, when shaken, spilled out several Lilliputian elephants, improbably carved by someone with remarkable manual skill. Sometimes he just brought a Pan Am bag or cutlery from the flight or a pair of leather slippers. The objects themselves seemed unimportant; but the giver of the objects was the father I loved, the one who kept in his pocket a list of our dress and shoe sizes, who didn't mind spending a little on his daughters, imagining me (I imagined) in an expensive teal sweater with buttons at the neck. But this was the father that didn't last long, an ephemeral father, the one who within minutes of arriving home, found fault. At home, plodding, practical, obsessively compulsive, enamoured of the minutiae of Jewish observance, descending the stairs of the Far Rockaway 'el' each evening with a face looking inexpressibly burdened, he'd complain about spending an extra dime, and would charge us a nickel for every light we left on. Every article of clothing we bought – mostly from the bargain racks at Alexander's or Korvette's – would have to be modelled for him and inspected by him; he'd check the price tag and the fit and inevitably groan. The beautiful, the sensual, the luxurious seemed part and parcel of his far away life, disappearing like fairy dust the longer he was at home.

The things my father brought from his trips for the most part lay around us unused or incompletely or incompetently displayed, as if my parents were afraid of making any connection with them. I imagine they liked and appreciated them but they disowned them, in a sense. My parents' attitude seemed to be: We have these things, but we hardly know how we got them. We are a little ashamed of them, so we don't display them, or make a fuss over them, or 'collect' them. I suspect it reflected their general discomfort with, their anxiety about, having money. They were of the middle class, citizens of a great, presumably stable country, but in their hearts they were the cast-out citizens of Anatevke, the fictional town of *Fiddler on the Roof.* And those people had nothing but an oxcart, the clothes on their back, Sabbath candlesticks and maybe a Passover *Haggadah,* the Jews' ever-present, ever-powerful narrative of affliction.

Creative Non-fiction Essay: Runner-up

Trina Beckett

One T Shirt Left

'You're only 55 once, Mum,' Fran had said. 'There must be something you'd like. Money no object – we'll all club together. A party maybe?'

When had I ever liked parties? Should I mention juggling skills? I couldn't remember where I'd read it, but wasn't it supposed to improve short term memory?

'How about something a bit different?' I'd suggested. 'Surprise me.'

They had. 'Rain Forest Zip Line Adventure, Honduras; the perfect way to appreciate the natural environment from a different perspective', the ticket stapled into my birthday card promised. My neck went red and blotchy at the childhood memory of sitting, petrified, in a tyre slung from a washing line at the top of the garden, too scared to let myself go whizzing down like all the others.

'Cowardy cowardy custard,' my elder brother had taunted .

'Scaredy cat. Scaredy cat,' my little sister joined in. Arrows of laughter stabbed me in the back as I slunk to the garden shed, curling myself into a ball of shame. They were right, I was a coward. Forty-five years on, I had learned to hide it, but nothing had changed. I picked up the phone.

'Fran...'

'Mum. Happy 55th. We all thought you might appreciate a bit of adventure for a change.'

How could they have got it so wrong?

'… Fran, I can't let you spend all that money on me. If you cancel now, you'll probably get a full refund.' My lips felt dry.

'Won't hear of it. Let us spoil you. Put yourself first for a change.' Exactly what I was trying to do. 'Must dash, got a tricky board meeting in half an hour.' She was gone.

Six weeks later, the ticket to a 'bit of adventure' was sticking to my sweaty palm as our monkey-motifed tour bus lurched off the Honduran highway on to a rain-furrowed, rock-strewn track, snaking its way deep into the fabled rain forest. A new vocabulary of green became my world. An assortment of Indiana Jones hats, khaki trousers, combat jackets and a curiously inappropriate 'I've Done Antarctica' T-shirt adorned my travelling companions. I felt out of place in my sensible thick cords and buttoned up sweat repellent top. Group bravado bubbled to the surface in the stifling heat.

'Thought I'd test the old hip replacement.'

'Hope the pacemaker is up to it.'

'Never wanted to die in an old folks' home anyway.'

'Getting proximity,' announced our guide, looking suitably impressed with his English. Proximity, just round the next hairpin bend, heralded a party of smiling, bouncy young men, raising their eyebrows like synchronised swimmers, as the cast of Miss Marple creaked off the bus into a bamboo holding area.

'Arnold welcome you. See pictures. This what you do.'

Jaws dropped in unified horror, bubbling bravado now a gentle simmer. Premonitory howling of exuberant monkeys ripped through the trees.

'Anyone like not do this. Say now.'

I opened my mouth and closed it again. His tone pleading, he tried again.

'Eight zipline, four bridge. Once do first, must do all. No fetch back.'

Silence. Next, a mime worthy of Marcel Marceau, culminating in what appeared to be instructions for getting out of a spin drier whilst tied up like Houdini. Ropes and ironmongery, more appropriate for an ascent on Everest, hung round glistening walls. No oxygen cylinders. Pity. I tried deep breathing but in the cramped humid cabin it wasn't much help, each inhalation haunted by the ghosts of fear past. Fear present was making its own unique contribution, the spectre of fear yet to come lurked in the wings.

'I'm not sure. It wouldn't be fair on everyone else if...' The 'Done Antarctica' lady blushed as she spoke.

'I'll stay with her,' said her husband with indecent haste. 'She has blood pressure issues.'

Maybe the Antarctic temperatures had kept them at bay. No-one else volunteered. Harnessed into a large nappy lookalike – could prove useful – I tagged along at the rear of the sombre convoy as it trudged its way over steamy paths.

'We here,' Arnold announced, displaying teeth like a row of ageing gravestones. I tried to curb my morbid notions, taking comfort in my cowardice. I was not going to do this thing. Curly beanstalk-like tendrils partly obscured a rope ladder, leading to a ridiculously small take-off platform, near the top of a dead ringer for a giant stalk of broccoli. Something exotic, with a long colourful tail, swooped with a mocking cry from the interior of the dense forest canopy.

'Bloody hell. Sorry, I don't normally swear,' apologised the 'I'll go first' lady. Repeating the spin drier mime, Arnold attached her to the wire.

'No undo till end. Understand?' Her trembling fingers looked as if they did. 'Go when ready,' he encouraged, giving her a gentle nudge towards the platform edge. Off she went, gyrating several times. She waved excitedly – or it could have been a panic attack – from her landing place on an ominously padded tree some distance away.

Last in line, I watched, as with varying degrees of reluctance, the condemned were despatched, like bygone money-changing tins swinging across grocer's shops. Me next. My yellow streak was on its knees pleading its case. I didn't have to do this. I would never see any of these people again. I could embroider a tale with enough detail to convince my family I'd done it. Coward *and* liar? Butterflies, as heavy and doom-laden as albatrosses, had panic attacks in my stomach. I recalled watching a video of Fran preparing to bungee jump, her face a mixture of terror and grit. Grit had triumphed. I heard a metallic click.

'Go when ready.' I stepped off the platform into an emerald time tunnel, the next tree approaching with menacing speed. Where was the brake? 'Splat' was the word I would later use to describe my less than dignified contact with the trunk. A monkey sniggered on the branch above, as a matinee idol hauled me on to jellyfish legs. At least when you bungee jumped you only had to do it once.

'Need relax more.' Understatement. 'Next line highest.'

Back to square one, except square one had offered the option of retreat. Spinning like a drunken ballerina, I collided with the next platform.

'Next line fastest.'

The tall man ahead of me took this one like an eel attempting to avoid being reeled in. I just managed a sneer before doing exactly the same.

The bridges, tightropes with overhead cables like oily snakes, added different challenges.

'Best no look down.' Best no look anywhere. 'Not can fall – harness got you.' So had a damn mosquito. I didn't have a spare arm to interrupt its banquet. Edging my way along the final tangle of rope and wood masquerading as a bridge, a cocktail of relief and euphoria engulfed me.

'Wish I could do it all over again,' said the 'I'll go first' lady, fingers still trembling, as she unhitched her harness.

'Me too.' Euphoria speaking! I glanced through into the holding area. I'd held a lot in the last hour: my breath, slimy cables, something unmentionable shortly to be released from writhing captivity in my gut, but most important of all, I had held my nerve. There was one T-shirt left. Yellow. I didn't buy it; the colour no longer seemed appropriate.

Poetry: Runner-up
Isabel Gillard

Venus of Willendorf

A small, squat woman made of stone and light
she bore our aspirations and our fears
in prehistoric days – and nights.

An accidental from a limestone cave,
a gift of water in a bond with time,
she was created by an ancient hand,
flint-knapped to faceless, crude obesity,
and polished till she tingled into life.

'Give us our daily bread!' we said, 'the lamb
(caught in a thicket maybe), bison, coney,
reindeer, mammoth, elk. Keep our frail feet,
that err on bog and mountain, that one step
from certain death. Give us,' we said, 'a child,
a treasure from your body. Give us life!'

Those who were answered magnified her power,
made her afresh in bone and ivory,
marble, gold, chalcedony, paint and prayer,
in spirit; fire, water, earth and air.

1st Chapter Creative Non-Fiction Book: Runner-up
Patricia Byrne

The Veiled Island Woman

Yellow and purple assault the eyes of the visitor to Achill in early summer. The gorse snakes up and out across hills dotted with clumps of faded heather. Primroses cluster at the foot of purple-rust walls and laburnum and rhododendron flower in gardens on the spine-road through the belly of the island.

From Mulranny, the approach road curves around the south shores of Blacksod Bay in an arc that resembles the overblown silhouette of a crow's head. Four miles out from Achill Sound – on turning the bend at Tonragee – a first-time visitor will be startled at the full-frontal view of Slievemore Mountain ahead speckled with shadows that resemble spots on a piebald horse. The mountain dominates the remote place and it is as if it wraps within its bowels secrets of the dramas that unfolded in its shade.

The many travellers to the west of Ireland and to Achill in the nineteenth century must have looked in awe at the yolk furze on mauve hills against a backdrop of the glowering mountain. Those who came were missionary zealots and proselytizers to The Colony at Dugort; Victorian travellers and writers; seekers of diamonds in the amethyst quarry at Keem; hunters of seal and grouse; stone masons and engineers; artists who set up their easels facing the mighty waves at the cliffs in Keel.

In the early afternoon sunshine of 16 June, 1894, the journey of those who came by rail to Achill was both novel and melancholy. Strange sounds reached the ears of the waiting crowd as, for the first time, a train curved its way through flat bog land along the sea shore to the remote island. Some freshly-cut banks of peat would have been soot-black, others tan-brown and criss-crossed with cracks like the wrinkled skin of the elderly who waited patiently at Achill Sound. In the event that any islanders had gone to work in the bogs that day rather than wait for the train's arrival, they would likely have rubbed the turf dust from their eyes and looked in horror at the belching locomotive hauling its lonesome cargo.

Most of those who waited had risen before dawn to make their way by foot and by cart from the four corners of Achill: from Dugort and Dookinella in the north, Dooagh and Pollach in the west, Dooega and Shraheens in the south. Many carried cloth bundles of bread and cold potatoes with tilly cans of milk or stewed tea. By 8am they thronged into the village and shuffled to the Telegraph Office to enquire when the train was expected from Westport. Throughout the morning they trampled over the bridge and on to the hill overlooking the temporary rail platform, soon swelling into a crowd of over four hundred.

Sergeant Scully worried that his battalion of constables would be unable to hold back the surge and enlisted some reliable civilians who linked arms – red faces puffing and muscles bulging – as they formed a protective ring along the platform.

'Move back there,' the Sergeant shouted. 'For God's sake, move back.'

A long line of carts stood ready on the roadway, harnesses jangling off shafts and cart wheels rattling on gravel. A stout brown-clad monk from Bunnacurry Monastery held aloft a black flag on a pole at the spot where the train would stop. Scarlet petticoats and white calico mourning-bands flashed in the crowd.

As the morning hours passed at a snail's pace into afternoon, many of the mourners would have quietly remembered the dawn scene just two days earlier when hundreds made their way to Darby's Point in the south of the island. They had gone with excitement – most of them young girls – to board the four hookers that flapped their sails out in the channel. They would set sail for Westport to board the Glasgow steamer *SS Elm* for the onward journey to the potato fields of Scotland. The oldest of those who made the trip was Pat O'Donnell, aged seventy, who was accompanying his deaf and dumb daughter to teach her the ways of migratory work. From the harvest fields of Scotland and England, they would send back money to help their families pay the rent and purchase seed potatoes.

At two o'clock the train finally shuddered to a halt whistling clouds of steam and belching a froth of vapour and grime. It was a sight never before seen in those parts and one that would have made the smaller children cower in fear that the monster machine might explode before their eyes. The covered vans were opened to reveal plain deal coffins piled one on top of the other. The name of each deceased was shouted out and relatives moved forward to claim their dead, the air filled with smells of animal dung, steam and metal. Many pleaded for the coffins to be opened so they could view their relatives one last time but were dissuaded.

The pack of people pressed forward and Sergeant Scully's officers and helpers struggled to hold back the crushing throng. Dr. Davis attended the weak and those who had fainted. P. J. Kelly of the Relief Committee moved through the gathering dispensing financial assistance to the bereaved.

'Will they take this back from us for the seed?' Owen Malley, who lost three daughters, asked Kelly when he was handed a sovereign.

Some were angry and bitter. 'Didn't Balfour bring in the seed rate after he came and now it's worse for us than it ever was!'

In less than twenty minutes the coffins of twenty-eight of the drowned were loaded on carts and a half mile procession started on the five mile journey to Kildownet. The mourners whispered among themselves stories from the survivors of what happened when the hooker jibed and capsized just short of Westport Quay.

'Did you hear that Mary McLaughlin held on to her sister's hand in the water as long as she could? In the end she slipped away. Poor Mary – she'll have Bridget's grip on her wrist for the rest of her days. God help her.'

The funeral cortege wound its way over Davitt Bridge, women clinging to the cart wheels and shafts, black flags waving in the breeze. Their destination at Kildownet was a piece of hollow ground yards from the shore and the sucking tide and within sight of the ancient castle of Grace O'Malley, the Pirate Queen of the West. Seventy men set to work and soon the air was filled with the thud of picks on stone and the ring of spades sparking off rocks.

It was close to nine o'clock when the graves were opened and the coffins lowered. The *Mayo News* described the desolation of the scene:

> *As the first shovelfuls of earth fell upon the coffins, the wild lamentation of the people burst out anew. Shortly afterwards the rain fell more heavily and a fierce storm arose, and the wind shrieking over the mountain sides and along the valleys of Achill seemed to wail in sympathy with the poor sorrow-laden islanders.*

Scores of carts drove off from Kildownet into the night leaving the dead behind as the lights of paraffin lamps and candles glowed from the windows across the water on Curraun peninsula. For many days afterwards, torn shawls, baskets, ribbons and remnants of clothing could be seen strewn at the edges of Clew Bay off Westport Quay.

Jim Lynchehaun knew many of the drowned and their families. The three Malley sisters – Mary, Margaret and Annie – came from the townland of Valley where he ran a small grocery business. Bridget Joyce and Pat Cafferkey had lived in Tonragee close to his own birth place. Catherine Gallagher was raised in Curraun where he had tended his father's sheep as a youngster.

That summer Jim was in his mid-thirties, five foot ten inches in height, a well built, dark-haired man. An official sketch the following year shows him looking straight ahead with bright, piercing eyes – an almost arrogant look. His shoulders were broad, his face square-jawed and confident, his appearance – it was said – modelled distantly on that of Bertie, Prince of Wales. Locals remarked that he had a peculiar habit of wrinkling his forehead in conversation as if constantly restless and animated and those who knew said that 'drink had a most disastrous effect on him'. In the summer of 1894 his was an unstable spirit in a community pierced with raw emotions of loss, pain and anger.

By the standards of the time Jim Lynchehaun was an educated man. Having attended the village school he became a class monitor and progressed to the position of schoolteacher. But his unruly nature and his propensity for binge-drinking ended that career and he absconded to England while out on bail for assault charges.

When he returned in the mid 1880s a dramatic change in the island's infrastructure was about to take place with the construction of a swivel-bridge at Achill Sound. The islanders had watched the startling sight of the enormous steelwork arrive by sea from Glasgow. Thousands of tons of stone were collected by locals from the island shores and hills and valleys. Jim Lynchehaun's father, Neal, secured the contract to build the approach walls and by September 1887 all was set for the formal opening of the new bridge.

This honour fell to the gaunt, stern-faced, one-armed Michael Davitt, Member of Parliament, in whose honour the bridge was to be named. He came with his wife of eight years – the American, Mary

Yore – who was said to have dispelled some of the depressive gloom and sharp spurts of temper to which Davitt had been prone.

'It would be cruel on my part to detain you under this heavy shower of rain,' Davitt told the islanders. 'It is on record the numbers of poor people who lost their lives in wintry weather when trying to cross from the mainland to the Mulranny shore ...'

The official party proceeded to the bridge and walked along the temporary gangway to the cheers of the drenched crowd. A regatta followed with Michael Davitt having the role of judge and Mary Davitt presenting the prizes.

It would be several weeks before the new bridge was ready for car and carriage traffic. The plan was that Father O'Connor, Achill Parish Priest, would be the first to cross on his side-car on 26 September 1887, but Jim Lynchehaun was not one to let an opportunity for self-glorification pass him by. The story goes that in the small hours of that September morning, he drove his horse and cart in triumph over Davitt Bridge, the first man to do so. He was a man with an eye for his place in history.

Within months of the bridge opening for traffic, an English woman was driven across by horse and carriage to her newly acquired estate on the northern edges of Achill. Her path and that of Jim Lynchehaun would cross with sombre and explosive consequences.

In the days following the tragedy, prayers were offered for the island's drowned in St Thomas' Protestant Church, Dugort, where one of the regular worshippers was Agnes McDonnell, owner and resident of the Valley House three miles away. Agnes was then in her fifties, handsome with a head of thick reddish hair. Her portraits reveal a soft, delicate expression in her sideways profile but her spirit was a determined and stubborn one which would later be described as 'a great firmness of character'.

Agnes had arrived in Achill in 1888 from her city home in Belsize Square, London, having travelled by mail train to Holyhead, by steamer to Kingstown and another train across Ireland to Westport. From there she went by long-car north along Clew Bay to Newport, then west to Mulranny where the isthmus separates the waters of Bellacragher and Clew Bay, and onwards by the rounded contours of Curraun Hill to cross into Achill. At Bunnacurry, half way across the island, she would likely have seen the tower of the Franciscan monastery a short distance from the roadway before turning right to make the final stretch of the journey northward through desolate marshy ground to her remote new home within sight of the Atlantic Ocean.

Agnes was described by her solicitors, Dowett, Knight and Co., London, as 'an English lady, although connected by marriage with one of the most ancient lineages of Ireland (the Taafe family)'. She had purchased the house and estate from the Earl of Cavan, a property of over two thousand acres, half of which was described as 'turf-fuel or bog'.

By the time the *Victory* sank in Clew Bay, bringing heart-break to several of her tenants in North Achill, Agnes had done extensive work on the Valley House and was undoubtedly proud of her achievements. The front door of her home opened into a wide stylish hallway and doors leading to the two main reception rooms. The handsome drawing room had two large windows facing out on to the gravelled entrance avenue and a windowed alcove opening on to a well-kept walled garden. Through the drawing room doors was the dining room with an enormous white marble fireplace. To the right of the hallway was the small sitting room where Agnes kept the estate accounts and records of tenant payments. From her upstairs bedroom Agnes would have been able to look out on the sea in Blacksod Bay that separated Achill from the Mullet Peninsula of North Mayo.

When she travelled from her home to St Thomas' Church by pony and trap, Agnes would have swept down the front avenue with the small lake, Lough Gall, glistening on her left, out through the white entrance pillars at the gate lodge to Valley crossroads and west by the sand hills that stretched away to her right as far as the promontory of Ridge Point. After travelling a mile or so she would have ridden by the golden strand at Barnynagappul, where the incoming tide almost touches the road, before descending into the village of Dugort and then along the laurel-lined avenue to the rust-charcoal stone church.

When the Rector, Mr Fitzgerald, led his congregation in prayer for the dead in June 1894, he would have stood beneath three south-facing stained-glass windows depicting crimson-clad figures in biblical scenes. If Agnes looked out the leaded glass windows on her left, she would have seen the stretch of countryside through which she had travelled from her home and, very likely, clusters of black-headed horned sheep grazing on the lands reclaimed by the nineteenth-century proselytizers who arrived in Dugort six decades earlier.

A white marble stone plaque of Rev Edward Nangle, the Founder of the Achill Mission and by then a decade deceased, looked down on the congregation:

> *He devoted his life from the year 1834 to the welfare of the people of Achill among whom he lived for many years.*

Directly across from the church was the unusual settlement of The Colony, built by the missionaries and standing stark in its straight lines of two-storey slated buildings on the mountain slopes. The settlement was constructed around three sides of a rectange, with the Constabulary barracks and Dr Croly's residence at the foot of the hill and the largest building, the Slievemore Hotel, running along the line of the mountain.

There would have been much bustle and activity in the area at that time as tourists and travellers flocked to Dugort, which had become the centre of the island's growing tourist industry. The visitors were collected from the trains in Westport and came to Achill to fish and to hunt, to cycle, to climb Slievemore, bathe on the silver strand and take snapshots of the Minaun cliffs.

As Agnes left the church service, it's likely that she felt apprehensive about what the drowning tragedy would mean for relations with her tenants – not least her most troublesome tenant, Jim Lynchehaun.

Within days of the Kildownet funeral, a letter to *The Times* announced the details of the Relief Fund for the distressed people of Achill:

> *Sir,*
>
> *As the Press has fully depicted the terrible disaster at Westport on Thursday last, it is unnecessary for me to enter into details. Up to this the dead bodies of 25 girls and seven men have been recovered, and two men are still missing. Each of these was bread-winner to a family, so that there are 34 impoverished as well as desolate homes in Achill today. Each of the girls would have brought home £8 to £10 at the end of the harvest season, and each of the men from £12 to £15, so that the*

magnitude of the loss for this single year can be at once seen.

Subscriptions will be received by the Bank of Ireland and the Ulster Bank, Westport, or by me, and acknowledged through the Press. A committee is being formed to distribute the funds which we hope to receive.

I am, Sir, your obedient servant,
E. Thomas O'Donel,

High Sheriff, County Mayo
Newport House, Newport.

Clouds of pain and desolation hung in the brightness of the Achill summer. Weeks passed, nights lengthened, and the Atlantic waves grew taller with every passing day, smashing fiercely off island cliffs. Agnes MacDonnell lived alone in her large house within sight of the turbulent ocean, unaware of the horror that would descend on her and her home before yellow vegetation once more signalled an island summer.

Short Story: Runner-up
Mark Wagstaff

Death Ride Girl

When that chick fell off the sky, man she was beautiful. The blackest swan, sailing on eagle's wings to dust. The inks, man, called her Death Ride Girl. But she was no rider: she flew. Arms wide, the blackest poetry, quick and gone.

I'm like some toad, man, in the rocks here by the canyon. No one comes without I see. They come over the desert, hours, man, to the show. Cars and trucks, kids and dogs barking in the back. They cook out, take fish from the lake. Drink beer on folding chairs. They *ride*.

When the show was built, man, I recall like yesterday: dudes in hats, yelling, chewing dude cigars. Big old boys in mirror shades; that smell of *green*. You couldn't see the sun for red earth raised all over. And the stars at night, man: drops of blood. The sound was immense. *Immense*. Big machines, man, ripping centuries out the soil; at night, I'd see the jockeys, shooting shadows, spitting whiskey on the flames.

And he came, the old sorefoot, from way on down the river, with his bones and beads, his eagle feather, his rattle song of sacred ground, of ancestors ripped and shredded by machines. Man, I liked *that*. Shaking his bones, saying: three days, three days to leave our desert. They laughed at him. I laughed. But, man, my laugh's better...

She was in back with Brownie. She didn't want to be. She wanted in front like Tom. But Tom made like he was reading the map and Mum and Lame-o let him. Like, who needs a map in a desert. 'Who needs a map in a desert?'

No answer.

'There's only *one road*.'

Caitlin was young; she'd've liked being with Brownie. But Caitlin was 'too young for in back,' whatever *that* meant. Susie glared at the dull, red hills as Brownie wuffed and stumbled round, landing hard, heavy paws on Susie's legs. Why couldn't the bitch lay down?

'Why can't she lay down?'

'Why can't you shut up?'

They let Tom away, like usual.

'If you taught her…'

'*Me*?'

'*Anyone*.'

'Teach Susie to shut up?'

'Teach *Brownie*.'

'She ain't talking.'

Susie tuned out. Mum and Tom weren't fighting. Just pretending. Being lame. But not as lame as Lame-o, driving in mirror shades. Tom first called him Lame-o. 'It takes getting *used* to,' Mum told them. 'A new someone takes getting *used* to. It's hard for him, too.'

'Hard how exactly?'

No answer. She answered Tom. She drooled at Caitlin's little wants. She left Susie hanging. 'Middle child,' Tom would tell her. 'Best forgotten.'

The only good to the day was seeing the show, biggest fair in a hundred miles. There were water slides. Water slides in the *desert*. Broncos. And that big old gut-snapping 'coaster where… 'That girl got killed,' said Tom. 'Right off the top, ker-*splatt*.'

'*Tom*.'

From the caves behind his eyes, something stirred with Lame-o. 'You know, every fair has fatalities. Maybe every coupla years. It's not bad safety. It's people.'

'Man,' said Susie, 'That sucked the fun outta *that*.'

Getting close to the trail of hotdog stands, caps and candy cane, Caitlin jabbed the window with her puny little fingers: want burger, want balloon.

'When we *get* there.'

'*Are* there.'

'We're not stopping at every…'

Caitlin's squalling took the lid off. 'Why can't she shut up?' said Susie, though her fight wasn't with Caitlin. She got scolded, and yelped as Brownie tumbled on her hand. 'Why do we *bring* it?'

'I was thinking that.'

Tom was half and half a good brother. He teased her, pulled her hair; she was too fresh and spiky now to tie to trees. He stuck paper parachutes on her dolls and flew them from the window. He hollered like a jackass when she looked at boys. But he stood between her and Mum's anger and Lame-o's stupidity. When Dad died Tom held her, made it right for crying. He wiped her face and told her she'd be pretty neat someday. But he couldn't say, none of them could, when someday happens.

Lame-o couldn't park. He couldn't spin the dirt and walk off like a cowboy. He couldn't glide the spaces, lazy hand trawling the window. He drove around and around: too far, too close, too in the sun, too near the dogs at the trees. Susie hid, embarrassed, as, cut on every turn, he lost space after space. Blond kids poked their tongues out, dads laughed; he did nothing. Like always, they fetched up where they'd begun, shunting in a gap a million miles from anywhere, Mum fretfully chewing her shades, looking over her shoulder to see out back, avoiding Susie's glare. Susie practised glaring.

And not *just* it took hours to park: they had to give Brownie her run. 'We could leave her with the other dogs.'

'Leave *you*.'

'We bring her for the *car*.'

'A dog that size make you think,' Lame-o nodded, thinking.

'But they'll just steal the car and the dog. They'll *kill* the dog.'

'*Susie*.'

'Most felonies in fairground car parks are break-ins,' Lame-o told the stunned silence. 'Not actual *stealing* cars.'

'So they'll kill the car and steal the dog.'

The rule was an hour family time, then fun stuff. Mum wasn't in love with the fair. She'd catch the sun in Kiddie Korner with Caitlin, who dived around in the sand and water, shouting, 'Look, Mummy, look.' Susie never got how Mum did that stuff with Caitlin; hadn't she lived it twice before? Lame-o sat behind his shades eating popcorn, ignorant of the law that you never eat popcorn outdoors. If he chanced a ride, he'd sit behind his shades and do nothing. He was the emptiest nothing Susie ever saw.

Tom came alive on the rides. That sense of him that was still a kid won out his teenage cool. He whooped and yelled the drops, the slams, the corkscrew twists. Too short for the hottest rides, Susie waited dutifully, till he dived her down the watershoots, barrelling the rapids. He'd hug her, pretending he was scared, like Dad would. Giddy on the waltzers, jammed on the dodgems, gleefully sick on the pirate ship, he'd creep behind the other kids, make pukey sounds so they'd cuss him. She ran with Tom, laughing, through the crowd; he'd dare her: 'Flip the bird at that fat guy.' Liberated, Susie raised her salute, and they'd tumble off, barking and cussing.

'I wanna go on the 'coaster.' She slurped her cola, so grandmas would stare.

'Too short, Shortcake.' He was conning round for where to smoke.

'No, the *old* 'coaster.' The bargeboard, hillbilly railway that dropped like a house from the sky. 'I'm tall.'

'Hey.' He'd seen a girl or something. 'Just gonna suck a sly one.'

'Can I come?'

'You *cannot*. Smoking olds your skin.'

'S'that what happened to you?'

He cuffed her ear. 'Once on the 'coaster and I'll be back.'

'Is she neat Tom?' Susie played up the little-girl voice. 'Shall I come see?'

'*Screw*.'

She didn't like to ride by herself, but he was kind and bought her stuff and, she thought emptily, deserved more for his day. It was achy to think how few times more there'd be with Tom. He was growing, didn't say so much about where he'd been. When girls rang his phone, he'd step right out the house. She was a chore for him now; she could see him make the effort. It didn't come natural any more: he worked to be her brother. He was thinking of college; soon he'd be gone and she'd be the eldest, with Caitlin and Mum and the poisonous vacuum of Lame-o. There was no reason Mum had him around. He'd attached himself to her widowhood like – 'Shit,' she said it out loud. Like shit crusts up a cow's hide. He slept in Mum's bed, on Dad's side of the bed. He was grotesque, hateful, setting rules and talking: 'Shit.' Breaking things he couldn't fix. Tom's friends, everyone, called him Lame-o. Scott called him Lame-o to his face; he did nothing. Susie hid, embarrassed, as everyone who knew Dad stopped coming by. The whole family died and Lame-o sequestered their bones.

The bar came down ahead of her. She'd have to wait next ride. Hot with the sun, Susie was sugar-gone sleepy. Her phone rang. Left it to message. Tom said, 'Be cool, leave it to message.'

'You getting that?'

'Huh?'

'Phone.'

Susie felt her pocket but the sound had stopped.

'Mine's got tunes.' The girl flicked a thin black cell. Some song played. 'Neat.'

Susie shook her tired head, trying to come alive. Her skull buzzed, like when she was a kid, Tom said he saw a bee crawl in her ear when she was sleeping. She banged her head an hour to pitch it out. The girl was maybe Tom's age, with a short, dark bob; round freckle face that looked kinda cool. She was all in black like the girls out back of the sly rock bar in town. The girls Tom said were jailbait, each time he went over.

'I love the 'coaster.' The girl jammed her hands in her jean pockets. 'More than the rocketship, the…'

'Starburst? Can't ride that.' Tired, she was sullen.

'It's dumb,' the girl said happily. 'They should do it by looks, not height. You here on your own?'

'Family.'

'Neat.'

'Huh?'

'Neat they let you off. My folks *never* did that, no sir.' She looked around. 'I was, like…' she pulled an imaginary leash and grimaced.

'I'm here with my brother. He smokes.'

'D'you smoke?'

'He says not to.'

'It's neat. So let's review: oldies in the sand pit, playing with baby brother?'

'Sister.' Vile, how lame she must seem. She could mix it up, though. 'He's not my dad anyway. Dad's dead.'

The girl popped with her tongue in the lid of her mouth. 'Quick, was that? Like, tragic?'

Yeah, Dad died a hero, in crossfire, winning the war. He went down, righting wrongs. 'He was hit by a truck.'

'Bummer.' The girl's voice was flat, but that was cool: she didn't know Dad. 'Must've been messed up, yeah?'

'They peeled road out his face.' She could say it and not feel the kick split her guts anymore. Maybe it was getting better, like the stupid priest said; when he sat her down with his cemetery eyes, all she wanted to say was: 'Shit.'

'Huh?'

Susie shook her head. 'I just like to say it.'

'Neat.'

The 'coaster clattered back down the ride; the line stirred, making ready

'Gonna wait on your bro'?'

Susie was peevish. 'I'm plenty tall.'

'Nah, I mean I'll ride with you. So you don't get next to some lame.'

'Lame-o.'

'Huh?'

'The guy Mum,' she spat it, 'dogs round.'

'Yeah? Already?'

Susie knew to the hour how long since Dad left. 'Yeah, already.' She went by the bar, feeling a rush of air as the girl pressed up beside her. She paid her token, the girl her shadow. 'You cheesin'?' she hissed.

'Yeah, man. I ride for nix.'

Susie went up head of the train, right where there was clear air. The chat and clatter of folks behind faded in the warm day. Not sleepy now, she felt in with everything: the hot leatherette of the old brown seats baked her jeans; the scalding metal grabs; distant fairground music; barking dogs, a tannoy voice and, somewhere, a buzzing phone.

'Hey,' said the girl beside her. 'This is where I love: top car.'

With a ringing shudder, the wheels awoke, surprised at the juice stinging through them. Susie clutched the grab, grunting where it scorched her skin, as the train began its rise on the steel-and-sleeper mountain.

'I been riding this *forever*. Since, oh, small, I guess.'

Susie gritted her teeth for the curve. 'Dad used to bring me. We sat here.' The floor dropped from her stomach.

'You miss him bad?'

It was shocking, uncool, *immense* to say how bad. 'Yeah.'

The train slowed, to speed again on the snake's belly. 'This Lame-o, what's he know?'

'Shit.'

'But your mamma steps to?'

Mum wasn't the neatest, thinnest; 'not the brightest,' Tom would say. But kinda cute and kinda right, and baked the creamiest pie. There was no explanation for Lame-o; he had nothing she could want. 'She likes company.'

'No shit.'

They stopped at the summit, a bargeboard platform of brush and cracked green paint. The rails ticked in the endless heat, crickets sang and, way below, a gentle rush like the sea rose up, the sound of the fair in the desert.

'Tell you,' the girl's voice, there in her head. 'You need an out.'

'This is my out.' There'd be no more, not till the far side of summer. Dad must've had money somewhere: he went to work in a suit. But since Lame-o, they had nothing: Mum spent evenings patching. Susie saw Dad's money some place, boxed, buried treasure. Get that, get out. Go with Tom, whatever.

'I mean there's better *rides*.'

The train clanked to life, speeding, going down.

'I'm too *short*.'

'Not to fly.'

Susie thought maybe the girl took stuff. Scott and the boys said they took stuff. That was cool. 'You mean *fly*?' Her words swam behind her, whipped away on the updraft.

The girl's voice was clear and present. 'I mean it. I can fly.'

'Since when?' They zipped round a curve, shaken against each other. The girl's solid body bumped her ribs.

'Since forever. I'm special.'

They were hurtling, getting nearer, straining for the drop.

'D'you wanna?'

She saw the girl's hand move over hers and they were locked together. The bony grip startled her skin, its strength made her shriek. But everyone shrieked; the noise broke up on the wind.

'C'mon honey. You'll know what to do.'

As the train hit its shuddering fall, Susie was soaring over the track, the fair, hand in hand with the girl. Propelled away from the 'coaster, they skimmed across the hot air, a sudden glorious breath of beginning consuming Susie's lungs. 'Wow,' she laughed. 'Look, Mummy, look.'

The girl's grip on her hand was fading, the onward force less sure. A drag began to tell in her bones, a faint hint of distant persuasion.

The girl's voice slayed her. 'Hey, kid: I lied.'

Susie saw her chipped, compacted face, her broken angel wings.

Man, that kid was the shortest thing I ever see dive the 'coaster. The noise was immense. *Immense*. There was sirens, man, and this big brown dog messing the flow. And the crying, man. *Wailing*. Them all, but the cat in the shades. He seemed pleased, like he wished it, brother.

And the ’coaster, she goes up and down her mountain. The inks say: How Many More? but they just selling stories. That old sorefoot, *he’d* tell you, with his broken beads and scavenged eagle father. But he’s long gone to the hunting ground to drink red eye with his dead fathers.

Not me, man. I’m like some toad. I stay in the rocks, here, hidden. I see the black mamma crow bring her babies. I see the fair, my friend, in my long and lazy years. Best show in the desert. If you wanna catch a ride.

Unbound Press Literary Competitions 2010

Results List

Short Story

1st Prize	Judy Walker	*All There Is*
2nd Prize	Peter Jordan	*Death and the Boy*
Runners-up	Paul Brownsey	*Human Relationships Under Capitalism*
	Sarah Crossland	*How to Date the Girl with the Middle-parted Hair*
	Miranda Landgraf	*Scotch Corner*
	Mark Wagstaff	*Death Ride Girl*

1st Chapter of a Novel

1st Prize	Louise Hume	*The Beginners' Guide to Parenting*
2nd Prize	Malcolm Bray	*The Resurrection of Danny MacNamara*
Runner-up	Laura Solomon	*The Theory of Networks*

Creative Non-fiction Essay

1st Prize	Seif El Rashidi	*Four Aces*
2nd Prize	William Prince	*A Writhing Mass*
Runners-up	Nicole Quinn	*We Killed A Nun*
	Moy McCrory	*Joan of Arc, Ringo Starr and Me*
	Desmond Meiring	*Pride and A Fall*
	Trina Beckett	*One T Shirt Left*

1st Chapter of a Creative Non-fiction Book

1st Prize	Ursula Hurley	*Heartwood*
2nd Prize	Cameron Dexter	*Death Divides Two Towns*
Runners-up	Amanda Montei	*The House with the Red Door*
	Ruaidhri Begg	*About Donald*
	Marilyn Messenger	*A Man of Stars*
	Patricia Byrne	*The Veiled Island Woman*
	Penny Wolfson	*Ephemera: A Memoir in Objects*

Flash Fiction

1st Prize	Gill Hoffs	*It's considered unlucky to kill them...*
2nd Prize	Phillip Sheahan	*The Tattooist*
Runners-up	Lunar Hine	*November*
	Michael Palmer	*The Birds and the Light in Pedro Carbo*
	Suzan Lindsay Randle	*Picking Up The Pieces*

Poetry

1st Prize	Annisa Suliman	*Ice etching*
2nd Prize	Susan Nyikos	*Inscription Found in Rilke*
Runners-up	Isabel Gillard	*Venus of Willendorf*
	Juliet O'Callaghan	*Under the Wig*
	J V Birch	*Apples and Endings*

Contributors

Trina Beckett lives in Cornwall and has rediscovered a passion for writing. She recently won first prize in a Writers' News short story competition and has had articles published in Miniatures Magazines, Travel Magazines and *Cornwall Today*. Her short stories have been highly commended, and she reached the third round of the Brit Writers' Awards. She works as a 1-1 tutor in schools and higher education. In her spare time, Trina enjoys coastal walking, travelling and playing the drums. She has been happily married for 35 years to military historian Ian, has two grown up children and three adorable grandchildren.

Ruaidhri Begg is the *nom de plume* of a published author who, because of the sensitive nature of this piece of writing, wishes to remain anonymous. Having spent a lifetime in business, Ruaidhri now devotes his time to creative writing and complaining about the weather.

JV Birch currently lives in the centre of London and works in Human Resources but her passion is poetry, snatching any moment available to create and indulge in this art form. Although city living excites, she plans to replace the fast pace and crowds with surroundings that are more natural and conducive to writing. In the meantime, travelling helps, with India, China, Iceland and South Africa among the most memorable experiences, providing useful source material too.

Malcolm Bray Having spent his formative years in Ashford, Kent, Malcolm decided from an early age that there must be other places. Discovering a similar mind in a girl from Boston, Mass., he brought her to the west of Ireland. Several years later he was attacked one night by the Muse, abandoning an outdoor life (forester, builder, farmer etc.) and launching himself on to the literary stage – well, he's won a couple of things and is in a few anthologies in Ireland and the UK. He has since completed three novels and two novellas, although short fiction is an on-going obsession.

Paul Brownsey has been a journalist on a local newspaper and a philosophy lecturer at Glasgow University. He has published about forty short stories in Scotland, England, Ireland and North America. In

Scotland his work has appeared in *Chapman*, *Cencrastus*, *Markings*, *Northwords Now*, *Cutting Teeth*, a Macallan prize collection and collections published by the Association for Scottish Literary Studies. He lives in Bearsden.

Patricia Byrne lives in Limerick, Ireland, and writes poetry, fiction and non-fiction. Her poetry collection *Unstable Time* was published in 2009 and her short fiction appeared in *Town of Fiction* from the Atlantis Collective. This opening chapter is from *The Veiled Island Woman,* a creative non-fiction book about an 1894 incident on Achill Island when a landowner, Agnes McDonnell, was attacked by James Lynchehaun. The incident became the stuff of folklore and the story was one of the influences on John Millington Synge in writing *The Playboy of the Western World.* Patricia writes a blog at www.patriciabyrnewrites.com

Sarah Crossland will graduate from the University of Virginia in the spring of 2011 with an interdisciplinary degree in fiction, poetry, and folklore. She is the editor-in-chief of UVa's do-it-yourself literary arts magazine *Glass, Garden* and also runs the lit-geek webcomic *The Library of Babble.* In her spare time, Sarah finds great pleasure in calligraphy, baking, urban exploration, rogue modelling, and the Criterion Collection.

Cameron Dexter, 24, lives in Lake Tahoe, CA where she works as a sports photographer for Squaw Valley International Ski Resort. Cameron grew up in Easton, NH (scene of her non-fiction work) and attended The White Mountain School in nearby Bethlehem, NH. She graduated from Saint Michaels College with a BA in Journalism and Mass Communications in 2008. Cameron's most memorable college experience remains her six months in London studying photojournalism. Aside from writing, her interests include skiing, sailing and photography.

Seif El Rashidi was born and raised in Cairo, Egypt. His work in urban preservation has led him to write about architecture and cities, and he tries to add a literary dimension to his writing whenever he can. Four Aces is one of his earliest pieces of creative writing (and his first published). He wrote it in 2001, but forgot about it, and only fished it out from his old computer in 2008, when he moved to the UK and decided to dedicate more of his free time to creative writing. He is currently the coordinator of the Durham World Heritage Site.

Isabel Gillard, a graduate of Edinburgh University, has taught English literature and creative writing in the Midlands for most of her working life, being for a time poetry-writing tutor at Keele University. She has edited several small-press magazines and anthologies, including the poetry quarterly, *Brimstone*; served on her regional Arts funding body and made a number of broadcasts. She has won awards for poems and short stories. One of her two novels won a small book of the year award and she has been pleased to break new ground recently with a memoir exploring a life-threatening illness – *Circe's Island* published by Unbound Press.

Lunar Hine In what spare time she can find from being mother to her 10-month-old daughter, Lunar writes, paints, and teaches free dance. Her writing always begins as short stories, but often condenses into flash fiction or poems, and in one case has extended into a novel. She is currently on a quest to earn what her family needs from these arts - you can follow her adventures at www.lunarhine.blogspot.com

Gill Hoffs, 31, studied at the University of Glasgow for her Psychology degree and worked throughout Britain as a residential childcare worker. She lives in sunny Warrington with her husband, a molecular biologist, and their son, Angus. Helping at her son's school by day and worshipping her laptop by night, Gill is working on a number of written projects including a novel for teenagers. Apart from a childhood letter to her local weekly about cats, this is her first work to appear in print. She once found plastic explosive on Dunure beach and tried to make candles, thinking it was wax.

Louise Hume is from Wakefield, but has also lived in Birmingham and Paris before settling in Brighton where she works as a historical guide and museum teacher. She co-runs Short Fuse, a monthly live short fiction cabaret night in Brighton and Hastings. Her published and performed work includes articles for magazines such as *Herstoria*, *Jane Austen's Regency World*, *The French Literary Review*, and *Orange Slices*, the fanzine of the band *The Wedding Present*. A frequent contributor to paragraphplanet.com, she is also published in two short story anthologies and had a play performed at the Hawth Theatre Crawley in 2008.

Ursula Hurley was born thirty-odd years ago in a grey market town in the Northwest of England. At the age of eighteen, she was lured away by the bright lights of Cambridge, armed with nothing but a copy of *A Room of One's Own* and an over-active imagination. Since then, she has written all sorts of things, including creative non-fiction, short stories, novels and poems. Occasionally she has even been paid for her efforts. She is based in Salford, UK and still suffers from delusions of making a living as a writer.

Peter Jordan was for many years a professional actor in both Britain and Italy, where he toured for several years with TAG Teatro of Venice. Fluent in Italian, he has translated two plays – *The Flatterer* and *The Gambler* – by Carlo Goldoni. He is a world authority on the Italian *Commedia dell'Arte* and is in the process of looking for a publisher for his doctoral thesis on the origins of the mask of Pantalone. Currently, he is Head of Acting at the Hong Kong Academy for Performing Arts. He is also very active directing, acting and composing music for the local theatre community.

Miranda Landgraf's fiction and autobiographical shorts have been selected for a number of anthologies, and her second novel, *Crash & Plastic*, set during the Iranian Hostage crisis of 1979, is supported by the Arts Council's Escalator Scheme.

Moy McCrory Born in England of Irish parentage, Moy's fiction has identified her critically as an Irish writer. Author of three short story collections and a novel, further short fictions have been widely anthologised including the influential *Field Day Anthology of Irish Writing* (2002), and *Irish Writing in the Twentieth Century* (2001). She was one of the featured writers chosen for the national short story campaign, *Endangered Species*, in 2004. She has worked as both a travel writer and an arts reviewer and currently lectures at the University of Derby.

Desmond Meiring was born in Kenya in 1924. He was schooled at Prior Park and Cheltenham College. In 1939 he was evacuated to South Africa. He was a police inspector in Kenya for 14 months, then joined the 6th South African Armoured Division of the British 8th Army for the Italian campaign. He was spinally wounded at Bologna but remained in Italy, and learned Italian well enough in his four months of hospital treatment to interpret with valiant northern partisans. Desmond holds degrees from Cape Town and Oxford, and has been a reporter with the Cape Times. Thereafter he worked for Shell International for 25 years, retiring as president for most of Spanish Latin America. He writes as a hobby and is married to spiritually-inclined blonde Soozi Holbeche.

Marilyn Messenger was born in Yorkshire, settled in Cumbria in 1988, and recently graduated from the University of Cumbria with a BA (Hons) degree in Creative Writing. She is attracted to life's quirkiness and unforeseen connections or consequences – if humour sneaks in then so much the better. Marilyn enjoys writing in different genres, but especially fiction, non-fiction and radio drama. She is currently researching and writing a book which touches on 19th century letter writing, amongst other subjects, and which has at its heart a small collection of letters between the astronomer, William Rutter Dawes and his wife, Ann.

Amanda Montei is a writer and educator living in Los Angeles, where she is an MFA candidate at California Institute of the Arts. Her work has appeared in Harriet, Nanofiction, Night Train, Dogzplot and others. She blogs for Ms. Magazine.

Susan Nyikos, born and raised in Hungary, teaches literature and writing at Utah State University surrounded by the western fringes of the magnificent Rocky Mountains. Her poems have appeared in *wordriver* and in the annual chapbooks of her local poetry group, Poetry@3. Also, she has been judging poetry for *wordriver* and the USU creative writing contest and publication, *Scribendi.*

Juliet O'Callaghan was highly commended for her short story, *In Arms,* in the 2007 Commonwealth competition. She has had two short stories published in anthologies. She is a psychology teacher and is married with two children. She is currently procrastinating over her 'third time lucky' commercial fiction novel: *The Physics of Madness.* Juliet enjoys writing poetry and flash fiction and aspires to become a published novelist. She reads voraciously and her favourite author of all time is Margaret Atwood. She is currently delving into quantum theory and multiverses and believes there is a successful version of her out there somewhere.

Michael Palmer grew up in Utah. He currently lives in Lubbock, Texas, where he is working on his PhD in English at Texas Tech University. His work has appeared in *Dialogue, Wag's Revue, The Collagist* and other journals.

William Prince is a university lecturer in the south of France, where he has lived for over 30 years. He has always enjoyed writing but has only recently begun to write short pieces. His previous writing resulted in a novel, *French Sally*, which was partly inspired by the demolition of the restaurant and café theatre he ran for some years before entering higher education. Written over a period of fifteen years and blending many different genres, *French Sally* was recently published by Unbound Press.

Nicole Quinn has written for HBO, Showtime, and network television. She wrote/directed/executive produced the feature film *Racing Daylight* starring Academy Award nominees Melissa Leo and David Strathairn, distributed worldwide by Vanguard Cinema International. Her short plays are published by Playscripts inc., Viking Vintage Originals, and Smith and Kraus. She is presently lost in the dystopic future of *The Gold Stone Girl*, a feminist fantasy. She is honored and awed to be published by Unbound Press. *We Killed a Nun* is excerpted from her unpublished memoir *Habit Forming*.

Suzan Lindsay Randle Originally from the Midlands, Suzan has worked mainly in the media. Her flash fiction and short stories have been published in mainstream magazines including Yours and My Weekly; teenage magazines Catch, Jackie and Shout; small press publications and on the internet. Her story Marooned appeared in the anthology *Jealousy* (Slingink 2007).

Phillip Sheahan was born and brought up in Australia but it wasn't until he settled in the UK that he started to write fiction. Theatre interests led him to writing for the stage – plays, sketches, performance pieces followed. Notable successes have included *Soapsud Island* an innovative reminiscence play written for the

Questors Theatre, London. Phillip also enjoys writing short stories and haiku and believes that the discipline of writing poetry is an excellent stepping stone to writing flash fiction. *The Tattooist* is his first attempt at the genre for a competition.

Laura Solomon has an honours degree in English Literature and a Masters degree in Computer Science (University of London, 2003). She has published two novels with Tandem Press: *Black Light* (1996) and *Nothing Lastin'* (1997). Her play based on her short story, *Sprout*, was part of the 2004 Edinburgh Fringe Festival. Her short story collection *Alternative Medicine* was published in early 2008 by Flame Books, UK. Her novels *An Imitation of Life* and *Instant Messages* are due to be published in 2010. Various other poems and short stories have appeared online and in literary magazines.

Annisa Suliman is a senior lecturer in journalism at Leeds Metropolitan University. Originally trained as a print journalist, she spent over 20 years working in news and public relations. A return to full time education in 1996 proved life changing. After completing a BA in English, then an MA in Victorian Literature (University of Leeds), she retrained as a lecturer and has taught at York St John and Teesside. In 2009 her poem *Fetish* won second prize at the Ilkley Literature Festival and she is currently writing a travel memoir. She is married, has three daughters and lives in York.

Mark Wagstaff was born on the North Sea coast of Kent but has lived most of his life in London and cities and their people form the heart of his work. Mark has been fortunate enough to have a number of short stories published and is also the author of four novels, including 2008's acclaimed The Canal. Full details of Mark's work are available at www.markwagstaff.com . His latest novel *In Sparta*, a powerful political story of radicalism and conformity, is available from bookshops and www.troubador.co.uk

Judy Walker lives in Northumberland and attends a weekly writing group in Newcastle, from which she gains huge inspiration. She won the UKA Opening Pages Award in 2007 for her first children's novel *Frankie*, which was published by UKA Press in November 2008. Her short stories have been published in anthologies and magazines and broadcast on BBC Radio. Her drama work has been performed in

Northumberland, Tyne & Wear and London. She has an MA in Creative Writing from Newcastle University. Judy is currently working on her second novel, this time for grown-ups. She loves baking cakes and collecting eavesdroppings.

Penny Wolfson won a (U.S.) National Magazine Award in Feature Writing in 2001 for an essay in *The Atlantic Monthly* called *Moonrise*, which has since been anthologized in several collections, including *Best American Essays.* Her memoir of the same title was published by St. Martin's Press in 2003. She is a contributing editor to the graphic arts magazine *Print*, for which she has written several features since 2007, including articles on high school yearbooks, radium advertising and on the history of letterheads, and where she now writes a column about family, memory, and ephemera.

Lightning Source UK Ltd.
Milton Keynes UK
06 December 2010

163964UK00001B/22/P